MAGIC-BORN

DRAGON

MAGIC-BORN
DRAGON

K.N. LEE

Cover designed by Danielle Fine
Edited by Genevieve Stutz
Formatted by Ashley Michel

DEDICATION

For My Family.

CHAPTER 1

BLOOD DRIPPED FROM ROWEN'S HANDS and between her fingers as she clutched her wound. The pain continued to throb and shoot from the hole in her hand where Siddhe stabbed her, to her shoulder.

Run.

It was all she could think to do as the fear of being seen and caught consumed her. Jumping over roots and rocks, her hair flew around her face as a breeze swept in from the sea. Rows of trees stretched out on either side of Rowen. Her eyes darted to every animal whistle she heard and every rustle of the trees.

Nowhere was safe. Not when she was on the run from the Withraen army, navy, or anyone else looking for the half-blood Dragon who murdered the prince. It was a false accusation, but no one cared to believe her.

Lawson.

Though it had been what felt like ages ago, her heart still ached for him, his kiss, and his arms around her when she was most afraid. Rowen loved him, and now he was dead. She still didn't know who killed him, but it no longer mattered.

All that mattered was survival.

It had been that way since she was a little girl.

Rowen would adapt. She always did. Need a meek lady-in-waiting? She could be that. A seductress to catch the crown prince's eye? She could be that too.

Now, as she ran toward the human realm, she knew what she needed to be.

Human. Plain and simple.

Rowen skidded to a stop on the thick grass and turned around, wide-eyed as an explosion came from somewhere far behind.

The color drained from her face and her heart thumped even harder in her chest.

Captain Elian's ship. It had to be what that was. He, Gavin, Siddhe, the other pirates had probably met a bitter end against the Dragons of the Withraen Navy.

Her heart sank into the pit of her stomach. She realized the man whom may be her father was gone. Just when she met him.

It hit her harder than she thought it could. Only hours ago had he called her daughter. The idea hadn't fully sunken in. All her life she'd wondered what her real father was like. As she suffered the emotional and physical abuse of her stepfather, the Duke of Harrow, she dreamed of what life would have been like if her mother had stayed with him.

Where would they be? What would Rowen be like?

All those questions were left unanswered, now as his ship lay in flames, getting swallowed by the sea. He'd saved her from an unjust execution and all she did in return was fear and doubt him.

The leaves of the trees rustled, and a flock of black birds cawed and flew above her away from the explosion.

Sighing, Rowen's shoulders slumped and she slowly backed away.

That was one relationship she'd never get a chance to explore, and she feared that if they did meet again...it would not fair well for her.

Hours rolled by as Rowen made her way along the edge of town toward the border of Harrow and Kabrick. She'd never stepped foot on human soil before that day, and always imagined what it would be like. Now, she might actually do it. All paths leading back were blocked. The only path left was forward.

A chill filled the air as Rowen glanced up past the canopy of trees at the darkening sky. Night would soon fall, and dressed the way she was, in a pair of Siddhe's pants, which were too long, and a tucked in blouse, she would not be able to survive the cold.

Rowen needed shelter, and quick.

Out of breath, she ran toward the open road. It was clear. There were no signs or sounds of any approaching horses or horse-drawn carriages. Just a smooth dirt path worn by years of travelers coming in and out of the port town she had grown up in.

The last rays of the sun faded as the sky turned a deep purple and blue mixed with traces of orange. Her eyes landed on the small inn across the road and the stable beside it.

It had two stories, and a white stone exterior and one large wooden door set beneath a long rectangular window. It looked empty, which was good. She just needed shelter for the night to clear her head and decide on which path she would take.

"You can do this," she whispered to herself. After all she'd survived, she wondered if it were true, or if she were truly delusional.

She looked in each direction to make sure no one was coming. All was quiet, except for the incessant chirping of birds and the soft hum of the breeze wafting her way from the sea. She'd be happy to never set eyes on the sea again.

Confident it was clear, she hurried across the rocky road and hid in the bushes. The stable was open, with only two horses hitched inside. She examined them from her hiding spot. They were fine horses, finer than she would have thought a small inn on the outskirts of town would have. Still, it was quiet, and as the horses drank from the trough, they cared not if she came in or stayed outside.

Rowen slipped in and covered her nose against the smell of fresh dung. It was strong, and the flies that hovered in the air seemed to note her presence, whipping past her face.

Her stomach churned as she searched for another hiding spot. There were four small stalls, just big enough for a single horse, a wall of hanging equipment, and a long wooden table. In the back was a small nook, packed with hay and hidden from view from the outside. She passed by the horses, and snuggled in. Finally, she worked at controlling her breathing. All the adrenaline from the day's events started to fade. Exhaustion took its place.

Now, what was next?

She rolled onto her back and looked at the ceiling. Whoever the black Dragon was mystified her. There was no reason for a Dragon to save her life, and yet it did. She wished it had spoken to her and given her some insight to what that whole rescue was about. Twice strangers had saved her. She sighed, hoping it would be the last time she needed anyone to liberate her.

She needed a solid plan.

There was no way she could go back to her home. Her stepfather would surely beat her for her failure. Or worse.

Thinking of what would happen made her close her eyes against the scenarios that raced through her mind. She almost feared him more than the thought of returning to Withrae, where they'd surely hang her the moment she was caught. If her stepfather got his hands on her, her death wouldn't be quick. He'd find a way to prolong her suffering.

She clutched her neck, swallowing a lump as she forced the memory of the noose away. There was still a bit of bruising on her tender flesh.

The stakes had never been higher.

Rowen gasped as a big brown mouse skittered past her feet and toward the horse stalls. She breathed a sigh of relief and turned onto her side away from the horses and the open archway. After a week in the prison tower of Withrae, she should have been used to mice.

She feared there were a lot of unsettling things she'd have to get used to. There was no one to protect her, now. Lawson and his power as the crown prince no longer existed. All she had left was her power to prophecize, and her ability to manipulate.

How far that would take her was unknown.

Her eyes closed and she curled into a small ball against the cold. Warm beds were a thing of the past. Just as she began to fall asleep, two big hands grabbed her by the shoulders and pulled her away.

CHAPTER 2

TODAY WAS A VERY BAD day. It would go down in history as one of Captain Elian Westin's worst, and as he bled from the mouth from a blow to the head, it could very well be his last. Elian's ship was burning, his crew was losing the fight for their lives, and there was no trace of the young woman he'd rescued to be found.

He didn't know what he would do if he lost his crew, and the young woman. It was a shame that his powers could only steal souls, but not give life back to the dead.

A female cry caught his attention and he spun around to see Siddhe jump overboard.

Siddhe.

He feared that finally...she'd left him.

It wasn't possible. They were bound until his death.

Was this it?

Did she sense that this was his last day and that she would be free to return to her kingdom at the bottom of the sea?

After years of wandering the world together, she might be gone forever. He didn't know if he would survive the afterlife without her. That thought broke his heart more than the fear of losing his ship. To have a heart broken twice could break a man, but Elian wasn't just any man.

He wielded his sword with the expertise his father had shown him. Still, it wasn't enough to stop the horde of Dragons that shifted and spit fire his way. With one hand on the hilt and one in the air, he closed his eyes and summoned the last of his dark souls.

Like black shadows, they were expelled from his hand and mouth. The smell of sulfur and coal filled the air as the sinewy figures were freed. Featureless faces looked down at him. Their hate was apparent from the pain it caused to release them. Still, they were his for one more bidding.

With a cough, Elian commanded them, sending them to battle the beasts in the air.

The calamity on deck reached a deafening roar as Elian's crew fought with all they had. As the sun began to be shrouded by the battle in the sky, Elian's sword was knocked from his hand by the talon of a Dragon.

Frothy waves crashed along the base of the Withraen navy vessel as a giant tentacled-creature emerged from the sea.

It roared, its large black eyes bulging from its slender, snake-like face.

The Dragons all stopped fighting, and turned to behold the sight before them.

Captain Elian stumbled to the railing of his ship and muttered a curse.

His eyes widened as he watched Siddhe ride the creature's back. She held onto the beast's ears, riding it like a soldier on a warhorse entering a battle.

Face set with determination, the seawater made her bronze skin glow beneath the clear sun-lit sky. Their eyes met and she nodded for him to get out of the way. Elian didn't hesitate. He also wasn't going to complain if a mermaid decided to rescue him. He ran from the top deck just as the sea monster swung its long, barbed tail at the Dragons.

This was it. They might actually make it out alive. He just needed one thing to secure his future. As he ran down the dark, wet hallway to his room, he heard the screams and roars of the Dragons on deck. A crooked grin came to his face. Siddhe never ceased to amaze him. She was one companion he'd be happy to spend an eternity with.

The grin was wiped from his face the moment he skidded into his room, and saw that the magic treasure map was gone. Countless maps littered the floor while some were still stuck to the walls. It didn't matter if his magical one was missing.

Heart pounding, he tore the room apart in search for it. Frustrated, and in a panic, he came to his feet and raked his hand through his hair. His eyes scanned the destruction of the room.

Where could it be?

Realization came to him like a splash of cold water on his face, chilling him to the bone.

Rowen.

His daughter.

Did the sneaky little wench know what she'd stolen from him? It wasn't just about treasure. No, it meant so much more to Elian—more than anyone could understand. His lips curled into a snarl. He should have known that she'd betray him. With a growl, he turned over his desk and raced from the room and back up to the top deck.

The Dragons had all shifted and were flying away, back to Withrae. What they left behind turned Elian's stomach. The men of his crew lay dead, gutted, dismembered, and scattered across the deck like rubbish. Siddhe and the sea monster swam to his side of the ship.

"Come on, Elian!" Siddhe shouted, reaching a hand out to him.

Elian stood there, frozen. How could he leave his ship behind? How could he leave his crew? Most of them had travelled with him for decades. What honor was there in running?

He gasped and stumbled backward as someone ran past him and leaped across the divide between the ship and the sea monster.

His jaw dropped as he watched Gavin hold onto Siddhe's waist and turn his gaze to him.

"Come on. The ship's sinking," the young man shouted.

Elian swallowed and set his face with determination. No use in dying.

Not yet.

He ran and jumped across to the sea monster, grabbing hold of Siddhe's hand. She was strong, stronger than any human woman and almost as strong as a Dragon. Without flinching, she pulled him up and he straddled the sea monster's neck. Siddhe wrapped her arms around his waist from the back and buried her face into his back.

"Let's get out of here," she said.

Elian nodded, and looked ahead as the sea monster swam with them toward shore.

"Where are we going, Captain?" Siddhe asked, holding tight.

"Kabrick," he said. "I've had enough of the Dragons for a lifetime."

CHAPTER 3

ROWEN HATED BEING MANHANDLED. SINCE the night of the prince's death, everyone ceased to treat her like the lady she had spent years training to be.

Her hands were pinned behind her back, and the fingers of her capturers dug into her skin.

She wished she had the strength to overpower the men who pulled her from the stable.

"Who do you think you are? Coming in here and sneaking a free night?"

There were two stable hands, one about her age and one older. The younger one kept asking her questions, to which Rowen had no reply. She was carried away from the stable and taken inside the inn. Her mind raced with excuses, but she decided to keep her mouth shut until someone of note questioned her. She would not waste her words, instead she would calculate the best response.

The innkeeper waited inside. He was a squat, older man with a bald head and white fuzz around his mouth and chin.

His sullen blue eyes looked her up and down as she was set before him. Rag in hand, he wiped a table one last time and stuck it in his belt under his round belly.

"What's this?" the innkeeper asked.

"Another scamp looking for a free stay," the younger stable hand replied.

The innkeeper rolled his eyes, his cheeks reddening. He held his hand out to Rowen. "Where's your coin, girl? We don't give out charity round here."

There was no way Rowen could tell the man that her stepfather was the duke of this village, and that they had enough money to buy the inn. Instead, she shifted on her feet and bit her bottom lip.

Behind the innkeeper a woman came stomping down the stairs in her boots. She was tall, with a masculine stature, broad shoulders, and a square jaw. She looked at Rowen, and then to the innkeeper.

"Girl," she said once she came to the bottom of the stairs. She placed her hands on her hips and shook her head disapprovingly at Rowen. "Where have you been? I've been looking everywhere for you."

Rowen's eyes widened. She wondered if the woman had gone mad and mistaken her for someone else. She looked behind her, expecting to see a young maid standing there, head bowed in shame.

The woman pointed to Rowen and then upstairs. "You. Go. You're supposed to be helping me pack up so we can get out of this fish-smelling town."

Realization hit her that the woman was indeed talking to her, and saving her.

Once again, Rowen couldn't help but think about how lucky she was.

When the woman stomped over to Rowen and grabbed her by the ear, she sucked in a breath.

"Come, now, you're slower than a mule with no legs," the woman hissed, and pulled her along and up the stairs.

She kept her head down and bit the inside of her bottom lip.

This better be an act.

The innkeeper and his stable hands went back to their work, and relief washed over Rowen when she and the woman reached a room and went inside.

The door closed and the woman let go, chuckling as she watched Rowen rub her ear.

It stung, but she could live with it. Nothing hurt more than the pain in her hand.

"Look at you," the woman said, looking Rowen up and down. "I wasn't much older when I was caught in the stables. My good deed for the day is done."

Relieved, Rowen nodded. "I can't thank you enough. I'm deeply indebted to you, miss."

"Call me, Feyda," she said with a smile that brightened her square-shaped face. "That was quite the night for me some odd years ago. At least I got this young man out of it."

Rowen followed Feyda's gaze to the slender young man standing at an open chest of garments. He nodded to her, but didn't smile.

"My son, Perdan," Feyda said, heading over to the wash basin. "And, you are?"

"Ro—," Rowen began, but cut off her name and snapped her mouth shut. Best not to reveal her identity. She had yet to decipher if she could trust the woman and her son. "Ro, ma'am."

Feyda dipped a cloth in the water and wrung it out. Then, she wiped it across her full bosom, held up by a tight corset and long, gray gown. "Simple name. Where are you from?"

"Just a small farm, not too far from Harrow's port," Rowen said. Her eyes went to Perdan who looked at her with distaste, as if she were a dead bird dragged in the house by the family dog. He turned his nose up at her and walked over to the bed, where more garments were piled high. She noted how his gait was graceful and somewhat feminine. With long blond hair, and high cheek bones accentuated by what she was sure was face powder. He wore a long red tunic and tight leather pants tucked into his boots.

"You're from a farm like I'm the Queen of Withrae," Feyda said with a snort. "But, it's okay. No need to give all your truths to a stranger. Especially one who saved you from a lashing and perhaps a night in the stocks."

Rowen pursed her lips, tensing. If the woman was going to use that against her, she'd better leave now. She did not want to owe anyone. But, being caught again was not an option. Torn, she stood her ground and listened as the woman went on.

"But, like I said. It's fine. I don't need to know your past. You might want to let me look at that hand of yours."

Feyda dipped the cloth in the water again and walked over to Rowen with it. Her eyebrows knitted together as she took Rowen's hand and examined it with her big, chestnut-brown eyes.

"This is nasty. I won't even ask how you got it," Feyda muttered, then clicked her tongue. "Perdan, fetch my tonic, would you dear?"

"Yes, Mother," he said in a voice much softer than Rowen imagined. He opened another chest and pulled out a black bottle and took out the cork. He handed it to Feyda and made a face at the sight of Rowen's hand. "What did you do to yourself?"

She lifted her eyes to his. "You think I did this?"

"Hush now, Perdan. She doesn't have to tell us anything," Feyda said, shushing her son. "What happened matters not. But, what lies ahead is what's important. Where are you heading, dear?"

Shrugging, Rowen watched her pour the liquid on her hand. It bubbled on the wound, and produced a white foam that stung. "I don't know," Rowen replied, sucking in a breath as the muscles in her hand began to burn.

Feyda tilted her head. She searched Rowen's face and tucked Rowen's hair behind her ear. "Well, you could come with us. We could use a maid to help us get things done. That way Perdan can spend more time helping me and not tending to smaller tasks."

"Really?" It didn't sound like a bad idea. A new life. Protection. How could she say no? Then again, she didn't know them and that made her wary. Too many times had she been tricked and betrayed by others.

"Yes. We both know you aren't the kind of girl to bend her back over a spindle or milk cows before dawn. But, we won't speak of it. Whatever you're running from, we can help you.

Trust me. I've been there. I was lucky enough to have someone to look out for me as well."

"Yes," she blurted. "I will come with you."

"Are you sure, Mother?" Perdan asked, folding his arms across his narrow chest.

Feyda gave him a sharp look that made his cheeks flush. "I am."

He bowed his head slightly in acquiescence and forced a smile for Rowen. "Then, I'd be happy to have you join us as well."

"Damned right you will. She'll be picking up your slack so you can learn the true trade," Feyda said and winked at Rowen. "See, dear. We all have a few tricks up our sleeve."

She gasped as Feyda puckered her lips and blew a cold gust of air onto her wound. The chill of it seeped into Rowen's skin and cooled her from the inside out. It stung, but she held her breath as the separated flesh fused together until the bleeding and the wound were completely healed. Rowen's eyes widened as she took her hand back and ran her fingers along the spot where Siddhe had stabbed her. There wasn't a trace of the wound. No scarring, just remnants of dark blood.

"How did you—"

"Shh," Feyda whispered, her finger held to her lips as her eyes searched Rowen's. "We both know how magic is frowned upon. Let's not discuss it here."

"Where are we going?" Rowen asked, even more intrigued by the odd pair. Her throat tickled and a tingling sensation raced along her skin, raising the tiny hairs.

Something told her this was more than chance.

More than luck.

Fate—that was more like it.

"Kabrick," Feyda said, turning to her son and placing her hands on her hips. "Time to leave this Dragon kingdom behind for a little adventure."

"I'd hardly call the humans adventurous," Perdan said, closing their chests and locking them.

Feyda glanced at Rowen. For a moment, Rowen was sure Feyda knew her secrets, just by the look in her eyes and the sly smile that rested on her lips.

"Oh," Feyda purred. "But, they can be."

CHAPTER 4

THE SWEET SCENT OF A fresh soul was almost too much for Elian to handle as he sucked it into his body. He shuddered at its entry and dropped the dead merchant in a heap on the side of the road with a broken neck and soulless body.

"Can you hurry it up?" Siddhe asked, keeping a lookout from the other side of the broken-down carriage. "We need to get out of here before Kabrick's soldiers decide to make their rounds."

Elian sat down on the road and closed his eyes as he became a bit woozy. He barely heard Siddhe's voice, or the anxiety laden within it. They were getting further and further from land, and that made for a very moody mermaid. She wasn't the only one in a nasty mood.

They were all out of sorts. Dirty, sticky, hungry, and tired. Climbing up the rocks of the beach hadn't been easy, but they all made it out of the battle with the Withraen Navy alive.

Well, not all of them. Elian hated to watch his men perish and his ship burn. He'd rebuild. That was all he could do.

While Elian calmed his breathing, his chest expanded with the fresh soul and he tucked it away with the others for safe-keeping. A surge of energy filled his veins and his eyes popped open. Springing to his feet, he unbuttoned his shirt and took off his boots and pants. The merchant was about his size, and had good taste. He ran his thumb over the ridges of the silver buttons. Very good taste.

Elian was more concerned with dry clothes and fresh socks to warm his chilled feet. Style was a bonus. It had only been hours since the sea monster returned them to land and they hiked from the beach of Harrow and into town.

Gavin peeked around the corner, his dark hair matted to his face. His eyes brightened. "Can I search the carriage?"

Elian lifted a brow. "What kind of pirate asks if he can steal something?"

Gavin rubbed his chin. "Well...I am just a scribe."

Rolling his eyes, Elian nodded to the carriage. "Take what you can. But, be quick about it."

Elian buttoned up his new blouse and tucked it into his pants. He threw a long red cloak over his shoulders, fastened it at the neck, and eyed the shining cane still clutched in the merchant's pale, white hands.

He tugged it free and ran his fingers along the rich mahogany.

Siddhe came around the corner and looked him up and down. "You look like an aristocrat," she said, scrunching up her face with disgust.

Elian flashed a joyless grin as he bowed before her. "Why, thank you, my lady," he said, sarcastically.

The corner of her mouth twitched as she gave him another once over and glanced at Gavin who had his shirt off as he rummaged through the merchant's chest of garments.

For a moment, Elian was sure color came to Siddhe's bronze cheeks as her eyes rested on the young man's naked chest. She quickly looked away and pulled herself into the carriage by the door handle.

"There has to be something in here that I can wear," she muttered. "If everyone is going to pretend to be upperclassmen, I don't want to be the dirty slave running behind you."

Elian took the merchant's money bag and slipped it into his pocket. From the weight of it, there was at least enough for them to be comfortable for the week.

Dry clothes, money, and a flask of dry red wine.

Things were looking up.

Still, he was absent one very important map, and one very clever daughter. He needed both if he was going to survive.

Elian walked away from the carriage and stood in the center of the road that cut through the lush forest. Just ahead was Billingsport, the port town of Kabrick.

An all too familiar pain stabbed him in the chest. He kept his balance and composure as his heart raged with a stinging ache that threatened to double him over onto his knees.

Instead of showing weakness, he walked ahead.

"Hurry it up," he ordered over his shoulder as he clutched his chest. "I need a bath, some supper, and more dark souls."

As Siddhe jumped from the carriage, dressed in men's trousers and an oversized shirt, which she tied tight with a belt and Gavin joined her in the merchant's slacks and tunic, he failed to mention one more thing he needed.

The thing he needed most.

Time.

Billingsport was bustling with merchants, sailors, and humans roaming the streets for their shopping.

The air smelled different here. Elian never liked the Dragon realm or its snobbish society. Here—even though he was weeks away from his birthplace—he felt at home. Wearing a rich man's clothes didn't hurt. Even though they all still smelled of sweat, dirt, and the sea, their clothes alone helped them command attention as they walked the crowded streets of the central marketplace to the local inn at the end of town.

By nightfall, they were well-fed, clean, and Siddhe lay naked under the covers of his bed. The Purple Blunderbuck was an inn he'd frequented during his travels. Somewhat clean, with an abundance of young sailors looking for a new opportunity. He always found a new pirate recruit during his stay. This time, the thought turned his stomach. Those men put their lives in his hands, and he squandered them away.

He left the open window and its sweet breeze. He sat on the edge of the bed while Siddhe slept with a faint smile on her face as her eyelids fluttered with dreams. He'd never been this close to the Red Dragon before, and the fact he let his chance for its treasure slip through his fingers was infuriating.

With an exasperated sigh, he pressed his fingertips to his temples. He tried to remember every detail of the map, and the new lines drawn by Rowen's blood. Images filled his mind as he recalled the last details he'd seen before the Withraen Navy interrupted him. Imagining the map was laid out before him, he traced over the newly-revealed route Rowen's blood revealed. It went through Kabrick and into the vast Wastelands that lay between Kabrick, Harrow, and the far, forbidding range of the Malcore Mountains.

That was forbidden territory, wild and uninhabitable. Traveling there without any direction could get them killed.

After a few minutes, he knew it was useless. Gavin memorized what areas had appeared before Rowen bled onto it, but he'd have to find her if he wanted the Red Dragon.

Fate was a cruel creature. To send his daughter, tease him with her power, and use her to ruin him was unfathomable. A knock came on the door and Elian reached for his dagger. He threw on a shirt and stepped to the door.

"What?"

"Sir," Gavin's muffled voice called. "I need to speak with you. If you don't mind."

Elian lifted the lock on the door and stepped out into the dimly-lit hallway. The smell of sweet cigar smoke and roasted lamb wafted into his nostrils. He winced at the loud roar of cheering that came from downstairs.

"What are they celebrating?" Elian asked, trying to make out what was shouted by the men below.

"I don't know if it's safe here. Everyone seems to know about our scurry with the Withraen Navy," Gavin said. "There are a bunch of sailors and pirates down there talking about it."

A smirk curled the corner of Elian's mouth. He placed a hand on Gavin's shoulder and leaned in. "We're safer here than anywhere else. Those men down there are human. They're probably just glad to hear of the Withrae vessel's sinking. It's not every day that Dragons get what's coming to them."

Gavin's brows knitted together. "No, sir. I think you have it all wrong. Those men down there," he said with a nod toward the stairs. "They are not celebrating the defeat of the Withraen Navy...they're celebrating your death."

Elian's smirk faded. Everyone thought he was dead. His eye twitched as he squared his shoulders. "Don't worry yourself about that. Get back to your room and stay out of trouble. We'll be leaving in the morning."

"Whatever you say," Gavin said with a shrug. "I just thought you should know."

With one last glance at the staircase, Elian nodded and stepped back inside his room.

He closed the door and pressed his back to it. What did he care if a bunch of dumb sailors celebrated what they thought to be his death? He had a mind to go down there, show himself, and consume all their souls.

No. Best to let the world think he was dead. That at least gave him an edge on his enemies.

And, right now, Rowen was at the top of the list.

CHAPTER 5

A WEEK WENT BY WITH Feyda and Perdan, and with each day Rowen started to question her judgment. The two were kind and giving, feeding her three meals a day and not working her too hard. She washed their clothes and tended to the horses when they traveled. But, their dealings worried her.

Feyda and Perdan always did business in back alleys, or under tables where no one could see their exchange of money and secret notes. Rowen only wished she could read minds. To know what Feyda had hidden up there would ease her own mind. She still trusted no one.

Despite her fears, Rowen kept her head down and her mouth shut. She didn't need any trouble, and if being with those two would keep her safe, she'd do whatever it took to stay in their good graces. At least she didn't have to worry about money, shelter, or food.

The trio never stayed anywhere for long, and she wasn't sure where they were heading.

North. Always north, but what lay there was a mystery.

Each night, Rowen rolled onto her side on the floor beside Feyda's bed. She kept the covers over her head and examined the treasure map she'd stolen from Captain Elian. It was in a language she did not understand, but one thing she did know was where it led: north. After years of studying, she also knew the geographical shape of their part of the world. Kabrick was key, and Malcore was where she had a feeling she needed to be.

She'd try to make sense of it all, and would tuck the map back into the front of her dress where it was safe, and fall asleep where visions of the Red Dragon returned to her. It was like a comforting memory despite the death and destruction her last prophecy had foretold. The Red Dragon promised to wait for her, and she would do whatever it took to reach him.

One evening, while eating supper in a port village named Chroix, Rowen overheard a name that made her blood run cold.

Rowen sat on the floor of the tavern near the fire, her legs tucked under her as Feyda whispered to a pirate captain and one of his crewmen. Her hearing was sharp, and there was no mistaking what she heard.

"No," Feyda said, her eyes widened in shock. "Tell me you're lying, Captain Blackthorn. I never thought I'd live to see the day..."

"That's right. Captain Elian Westin is dead. Sunk by the Withraen Navy right off the coast of Harrow," Captain Blackthorn. "Can't say that I didn't see that one coming. He had a list of enemies as long as the red road to Reeds."

"Shark bait," the crewman said with a laugh, his bony cheeks tight with a wide grin. "That's what he and his crew are right now, right Captain?"

Captain Blackthorn shot him a glare. "Shut it, Grimble."

Grimble's smile faded and he lifted his heavy mug to his bearded mouth. He downed its contents and slammed it onto the squat, wooden table.

Rowen quickly looked away as Captain Blackthorn's eyes rested on her bosom. She folded her arms across her chest and fixed her gaze on the fire.

"What's her story?" he asked, Feyda.

Rowen couldn't resist another glance back.

Feyda took his face into her hands and turned it back toward her. "None of your business," she hissed with such venom that Rowen tensed.

A chuckle came from his lips. "Fine," he said. "I just thought we were sharing is all. Haven't seen breasts that ripe in weeks."

Feyda stood. She turned to Rowen. "Come, girl. We have to be up early, let's prepare for bed."

Captain Blackthorn stood as well. The room went quiet and Rowen swallowed as he towered over them. With the build of a Dragon, it was hard to believe the man before them was only human. He had crystal-clear blue eyes and dark wavy hair that reached his shoulders. Dressed in all black, and with a scar going across his neck, he looked sinister. Even more sinister than Captain Elian.

"But, you haven't paid me for my information," he said, his eyes locked with Rowen's.

Feyda stood in front of Rowen, shielding her. She tossed a coin purse on the table. "There's your payment. Now, put your eyeballs back in your head before I claw them out with my fingernails."

Rowen's eyes widened. Where Feyda got the nerve to speak to the captain like that was beyond her, but along with fear of retaliation, she was also proud that this woman was her master.

Princess Noemie of Withrae wasn't even bold enough to speak to a man that way. Let alone a feared pirate.

Blackthorn slapped the tabletop, and Rowen jumped. Instead of yelling at them, he flashed a grin and snatched the coin purse from the table. Without another word, he and Grimble left the tavern.

When Feyda turned to Rowen, she noticed that the woman was visibly shaken despite her hardened demeanor and words to the captain.

"Ro, get Perdan. We need to leave this town tonight."

Nodding, Rowen hurried away. The sense of urgency filled her with adrenaline. She didn't want Captain Blackthorn storming into their room that night, and wasn't too confident that Feyda or Perdan could fight him off.

She hadn't been so afraid since she escaped Captain Elian's ship. When did fear become such a common occurrence? Rowen wrung her hands, searching the tavern for Perdan's familiar face. If only Prince Lawson was still alive, all her troubles would be over. Remembering him was too painful, so she shoved the image of his handsome face from her mind and focused on the matter at hand.

The tavern's air was thick with cigar smoke and the scent of sweat and ale. The floor was slick with the dark liquid. It was dimly-lit, with only candles on the tables and torches on the beams that held up the ceiling. In this part of town, beauty was more of a curse than an asset. Rowen could have easily joined the local brothel if she were desperate. But, since she did not plan on whoring herself out to the dirty men who frequented the pleasure houses, she kept her head covered, and her eyes down. It was easier that way, but sometimes she was spotted, and like wolves, the men chased her with their grubby hands and lude remarks.

Rowen ignored their comments, and like a ghost, she managed to glide through the tavern with grace, untouched. At the back was an archway that connected the tavern to the brothel, Rowen paused.

The women inside wore little more than their undergarments. Their makeup was exaggerated. Red lips and false lashes glued to their own, they were more like works of art than real people. But, the men they tended to were real enough, and Rowen spotted one with a black eye. Though she tried to hide it under powders and creams, Rowen knew one when she saw it.

Afraid to step inside, Rowen held onto the wooden pillar as her eyes rested on Perdan. He flirted with a young man who sat on his lap. She was surprised that the brothel had both male and female whores, and the deep reddening of her cheeks displayed it for all to see.

"Perdan," she called, softly.

He turned to her, his dull blue eyes glossy with intoxication. "What is it?"

"Feyda asked for me to find you. There's trouble and we need to go. Right now."

She watched him kiss the man on the lips and lift him from his lap. Grabbing his shining wooden cane—more for fashion than necessity—Perdan smoothed his long blond hair and shirt.

"Well, let's get going," he said, standing with an air of nobility about him.

Rowen knew nobility, she'd grown up as part of its ruling class. Perdan and Feyda were good at pretending, and she'd keep her mouth closed as long as they kept her safe.

"So," he said, hooking his arm around Rowen's. "What's the bloody fuss all about? What did my beloved mother get us into?"

Rowen exhaled. "Captain Blackthorn. He seems like trouble. I think she just wants to be careful."

"Ah," Perdan said, nodding. "Now, that's the kind of man you don't want to cross. Looks like we'll be traveling by moonlight."

He looked down at Rowen, with adoration now that she'd proven herself to not be any trouble, and a hard worker. Somehow, over the past week, they'd become friends.

"He saw you, didn't he?"

Rowen nodded and licked her lips. "I knew I should have stayed in the room."

"But why? You're too nosy for that," he said.

"I am not!"

He chuckled. "You don't think mother and I don't notice how suspicious you are. You're always listening, always watching with those storm-colored eyes of yours. But, we don't mind. We've nothing to hide, little Ro."

Rowen hated that he brought up her gray eyes. Lawson used to say the same thing. He'd call them the color of a storm. "You can't blame me for staying alert. A girl has to."

"Right you are," Perdan said, opening the tavern door. "Right you are."

They made it out of the tavern and into the night. Soft raindrops fell onto them and Rowen was glad to have a hood on her cloak. Before long, it would be soaked through if they didn't make it to the inn and pack up their things.

The streets were still bustling, as the night was still young. Rowen held tight to Perdan's arm and together they crossed the stone roads to the two-story inn just behind the statue of King Olwen of Kabrick.

Her eyes went straight to the statue's and it reminded her of the Dragon statues throughout Withrae. Having grown up there since birth, she didn't miss it. If she could return and free her mother from that place, she would.

The Red Dragon could solve all her problems.

Perdan paused just beside the statue. He held tight to Rowen and she looked up to see his eyes narrowed. "Wait here," he said in a whisper.

Warnings flooded Rowen as Perdan left her behind. A scream came from inside the inn, and Perdan broke into a sprint. To Rowen's surprise, he slid the cover of his cane off to reveal a shining skinny, silver sword. She stepped back, hoping to find cover behind the statue.

"There you are," Captain Blackthorn said, and Rowen spun around to face him. "I was looking for you."

Her heart pounded in her chest as she stepped away. He was accompanied by three more pirates, and from the sounds of the calamity within the inn, he had more with him.

"Be a nice girl and come here," he said, his grin flashing in the dark. Dark eyes and even darker intentions, Rowen shook her head.

"What do you want?" She asked, though her imagination could come up with a few ideas that turned her stomach.

He stopped and held his arms out. The moon's light reflected off the dagger inside his cloak and the hilt of the sword on his hip.

Rowen wasn't one for weapons. Her hands. They were her only protection. She shook. After failing to use her power on Gavin, she was now uncertain if that could help her now.

"You, princess. Just you," he purred, and before he could take another step, Rowen turned and darted across the street.

She pumped her arms, and her cloak fell from her head revealing her strawberry blond hair as she ran into the inn. Inside, pirates tore through the place, and Feyda and Perdan were nowhere to be seen.

Rowen abandoned her idea to find them, and grabbed hold of the first pirate to cross her path. He flinched and opened his mouth to shout at her.

It was too late. With one touch, he belonged to her. Her ability to strip away the will of her prey was all she had, and she used it without a second thought.

Her brows arched as she quickly spoke her command. Her power—hot and pulsating—surged from her belly, up her arms, and into the palms of her hand. With a silent jolt, the power shot into the pirate in waves.

"Kill Blackthorn," she said, and released him to run back outside.

Faster than Blackthorn and armed with a power he could never understand, Rowen ran from the inn as the pirate pushed Blackthorn into the street and raised his ax.

Rowen glanced over her shoulder to see Blackthorn stab the pirate in the gut.

Her eyes widened.

She should have chosen a bigger pirate, or one with better fighting skills. As she turned the corner, hands reached out to her.

"Feyda," Rowen breathed with relief.

Feyda grabbed her by the hand and Perdan motioned for them to follow him down the back alleyway.

"Hurry," he said. "I set a trap in the inn. It'll keep the pirates busy, but not for long."

Rowen followed, her legs burning as they all ran at full speed to their cart and horses at the end of the alley.

"Just a little something Mother used to warn me not to use when I was a kid," he said. "It's called the Spell of Discord. Very handy, it is."

"Enough chatter," Feyda warned. "Get us out of here. Take the Reed route to Billingsport."

Perdan nodded and once they reached the cart, he helped Rowen and Feyda inside and jumped in the seat up front to navigate the horses.

Rowen leaned her back against the seat and tilted her head back to get as much air into her lungs as possible. Feyda handed her a flask of water and pulled a thick red blanket over herself, snug on a long cushion that ran along the side of the inside of the cart.

Rowen drank it down and coughed when she realized it wasn't water. Her tongue stung and she scrapped whatever it was off with her nails. It was too late, the liquid rushed down her throat and into her belly.

"Yuck! What is this?"

Feyda took the flask and drank the rest down. "It isn't that bad. Just a little something to keep you awake. We all need to be alert. We have quite the journey and the roads are not safe."

Groaning, Rowen pulled her legs onto the seat and into her chest.

This was the life of a fugitive. She was now certain that she would never be able to stop running.

Not without the Red Dragon.

CHAPTER 6

ROWEN PRAYED THAT THEY'D MAKE it to dawn. She recounted old poems she'd learned during her years of boarding schools and academies. It was a comfort to remember the better times of her past, when she was free from the Duke's scrutinizing eye.

Hours went by as the elegant covered cart rolled along the dark back roads away from Chroix, toward Billingsport, her heart didn't stop racing. Whatever concoction Feyda gave her kept her on the edge of her seat. Sleep was a distant memory, and she was on edge, ready for whatever came their way.

"Calm yourself, Rowen," Feyda said. "No pirate or bandit is going to harm us. I've enchanted the cart's cover to make us look like poor farmers. Do not worry."

"They why give me the potion?"

"I just need you alert in case we do have trouble. Perdan and I can protect ourselves, but now, we have a young charge to look after. Can't have you ripped apart by Blackthorn and his men."

Rowen swallowed. Why didn't she just stay in the room? This was all her fault. She wrung her hands and kept an eye on the still forest outside the carriage window.

"Where are we going, Feyda?"

Feyda pulled her shawl close. "Further inland. Kabrick is a big kingdom, but Perdan and I have business near Malcore."

Rowen lifted a brow. "Malcore? The Wastelands?"

Silently, Feyda nodded. She watched Rowen, a hint of a smile on her lips. "Ever been?"

She hadn't, but she'd seen Malcore marked on the map to the Red Dragon. This was perhaps the best decision Feyda had made that week. At least she was getting closer to her goal. She just wondered when she'd find a chance to sneak away from them and continue her journey alone.

"I haven't. Just heard about it is all."

"I see. Do a lot of studying geography as a farm girl?"

Rowen shot a look at her. Feyda knew more than she let on. "I didn't say that. I just heard about it."

"Where are your parents, Ro? You never talk about them."

The question caught Rowen off guard, but she was quick to reply.

"Dead."

"I'm sorry, Dear," Feyda said, softly. "That must be hard for any young woman. To be alone in the world. I think fate brought us together. Don't you?"

Fate. Rowen was familiar with it. She'd never seen Feyda or Perdan in her prophecies. "I suppose it's possible," she said.

Leaning forward, Feyda lowered her voice as her eyes narrowed and met Rowen's. "Indeed. Anything is possible. I learned that ages ago when my mother brought my father back from the dead when I was just a girl of fifteen. It was a miracle."

"Incredible," Rowen said, interested in learning more.

Feyda shrugged with a sigh and sat back. "Didn't last though. His skin turned to mush and he fell head first into the fireplace that night. I can still smell his flesh burning in my dreams," Feyda whispered, scrunching up her nose as she looked far off.

Rowen's brows rose. "Really?"

Feyda nodded. "That's right. I was born with the gift of healing and other small powers. Necromancy was my mom's thing. Not that she was the best at it."

"So," Rowen began. "You come from human sorcerers?"

"That's right," Feyda said. "And, you're half Dragon, correct?"

Rowen made her face unreadable. She was good at hiding her true feelings, but her insides burned with fear of being found out.

"Listen, Ro. We found you in the Dragon realm. It doesn't take a master scholar to figure out you are half human and half Dragon. I can tell by your skin that you're not full-blooded, and human girls don't go across the realm's border. I just want you to understand that we don't care one tiny bit about your past. But, if we're going on this journey together, you should feel safe enough to tell me about yourself. No one is going to fault you or hurt you for your past. Not while I'm around. Understand?"

Tears stung Rowen's eyes, but she kept a blank expression. Instead of replying, she simply nodded and looked away. Could she truly believe Feyda's words? They sounded nice, and even made her want to spill her secrets. But, Rowen knew better.

Memories of Brea—her best friend from Withrae Castle— testified against her to the Dragon court. The betrayal stung like a knife to the heart.

Never again would she let anyone get that close.

"Billingsport is our final stop before we head toward the Wastelands," Feyda said to herself as she pulled out her journal and looked through it.

The carriage stopped. Rowen and Feyda exchanged glances, and then both leaned toward the side window to look outside. They pulled the curtains aside and looked out to a dark and dismal early dawn. The grass was wet with rain and mud, and a sullen-looking building of stone, wood, and hay stood before the cart.

"Goodness gracious," Feyda said. "We're here." She slapped the side of the cart. "Well done, Perdan."

He hopped to the ground. "I do what I can," he said, stretching his long arms over his head with a yawn. "Can't let dirty pirates snatch our little Ro from us."

With a breath of relief, Rowen sunk into the seat.

"He probably gave the horses a bit of that potion," Feyda said with a wink. "I raised him well."

Perdan opened the door to let them out.

"We made it," Perdan said. He held a hand out to help Rowen to the ground.

She jumped down and looked at the inn before them. There was a dark stable just inside the stone enclosure. An old staircase led from the ground to the second floor.

"The Purple Blunderbuck?" Rowen read the words on the sign outside on the stone wall that enclosed the inn in a square.

"That's right. Top quality lodging in this part of the realm. We've stayed here many times," Feyda said. "Good ole' Harold will make sure we're comfortable during our stay."

"Hopefully, it won't be for long," Rowen mumbled. She just wanted to get back on the road and put as much distance between them and Blackthorn as possible.

"Why?" Feyda asked, standing in front of Rowen with her hands on her hips. "You have somewhere to be that I should know about?"

"No," she muttered. The sky turned gray as dawn approached. The early song of a pack of birds in the birch trees filled the quiet morning.

"Good," Feyda said after checking her journal. She closed it and tucked it into her belt. "I need you to go to the cartwright shop and get me some more frost-weed for my rain charm. I need to enchant the cart's canvas cover before we leave."

"Which shop?" Rowen frowned as she looked to the path that led around the inn and into the quiet town. The last time she was sent to a shop, she came back accused of murdering the man she loved.

"The first one on the right. Don't worry. I know the owner. The cartwright wakes up early and opens the shop at dawn," Feyda said. She rummaged through her coin purse and handed Rowen two silver coins. "Give him this and ask for a bushel of frost-weed."

"Can't you go?"

Feyda lifted a brow, and tilted her head. "Again, do you have somewhere else to be?"

"I just don't want to go alone. I don't know this place."

"You'll be fine. Do as I say. I don't want to hear another word out of you."

With a groan, Rowen closed her fist over the coins and pulled her cloak's hood back over her head. The sun had barely come up, but she was off on an errand. She couldn't, and probably shouldn't complain. Perdan and Feyda had done a lot for her. Still, the tension from the night before lingered, and she was on alert for any suspicious men in town.

The town of Billingsport was smaller than Croix, with less rowdy sailors and pirates. Or so it seemed. It was early, there would be much to discover throughout the day. Still, it was a good sign that they were more inland, and perhaps safe from the likes of Blackthorn.

There was a central square with villagers setting up to sell their goods for the day. As Rowen turned the corner from the back of town, it reminded her of the little village near her childhood home in Harrow. Once a week, Rowen's mother would take her there to shop for new ribbons and bows for her hats and dresses. Even the scent in the air brought back memories. The smell of fresh bread came from a small building at the end of the road with a chimney that pumped a thin line of smoke into the air. Her stomach grumbled and reminded her that she hadn't had any supper. Perhaps if she finished her errand quickly enough, she'd be able to buy some for Feyda and Perdan.

She smiled as she watched a father pick his young daughter up and place her on his shoulders. She giggled and held onto his ears. Such a thing was foreign to Rowen. Her stepfather barely ever revealed a genuine smile to her, and the pirate, Captain

Westin, most certainly wanted her killed. She sighed, and her smile faded.

It seemed that the whole world wanted her dead.

Once she stood in front of the shop, she noticed that the wooden door was ajar. She peeked her head inside.

"Hello? I'm looking for the cartwright who owns this shop," she called as she pushed the door open to nothing but silence. Stepping inside, she looked around for any traces of the shopkeeper.

There was a forge at the far right of the room, and all sorts of hooks and horseshoes hung from the rafters of the ceiling. Shelves with wooden boxes and small crates lined the walls, and yet there was no trace of the owner.

"Feyda sent me."

A creaking of the floorboards caught her attention, and before she could blink, the door was slammed shut and she was grabbed by the shoulders and pressed against it by two strong hands.

"Hello, love," a familiar voice said. Deep, husky, and melodic enough to make any woman swoon.

Rowen found herself frozen into submission. Her eyes widened as he pressed his body against hers. He pressed his lips to hers in a bruising, yet passionate kiss.

She held her breath. There was something odd about his kiss. It wasn't offensive or vulgar. There was a deep-seeded affection there that caught her completely off guard. Enchanting green eyes looked back at her from beneath dark lashes. He smelled just as she remembered him, too intoxicating to be natural, with a disarming touch. He was even more handsome than when she'd last seen him in the Dragon court. His beard was gone.

Now, smooth sun-bronzed skin was revealed on his square jaw. He kissed her gently on the forehead.

Not even Lawson's touch had elicited such wild desire within her, and the thought alone confused her.

She licked her lips and swallowed as she placed her hands on either side of his face—to feel if he was real.

This was the man she hated. The man who accused her of awful deeds. Yet, a part of her was relieved to be in his arms.

She spoke softly, desperate to not withdraw from his soothing, powerful grasp.

"Prince Rickard?"

CHAPTER 7

JUST WEEKS AGO, PRINCE RICKARD had threatened to seduce her on a daily basis. Now that his hands glided up her arms and along the back of her neck, it was more of a lovely promise that she wished she could resist.

"That's right," he said and looked up from her eyes to her hair as he ran his fingers through her tangles. "What have they done to you? Are those humans not treating you well?"

Rowen frowned at the mention of Perdan and Feyda. "How do you know about the humans?"

He pressed his forehead against hers and lowered his voice to a whisper. "Have you not figured it out, yet, my clever little half-blood?"

Why was he being so tender? His brother was dead, and he accused her of doing it. He had every reason to drag her from the shop and back to Withrae where she'd suffer the hanging she'd been sentenced to.

Fear rose in her throat as she looked at him. She knew him to be sly, and calculating. Every action could be false, and she refused to fall for it.

"What game are you playing, Rickard? Why are you here?"

That grin she knew all too well came to his lips. He tilted his head and searched her eyes. "Come on. Don't pretend to be the victim. You've always been good at that, but I could see right through you from the start."

"I don't know what you're talking about."

He lifted her by her thighs and pressed her back into the door. He was so close that she could feel his heart beating against her own. His voice lowered to a soft drawl that made her skin prickle with need.

"You think you're the only one with secret ambitions. I've been masterminding greater schemes than you can ever dream of. Tell me, you've figured it out by now, haven't you? Show me you're much cleverer than any ever gave you credit for."

Rowen swallowed, hypnotized by his gaze and weightless in his arms. "I've been too busy trying not to get kidnapped, tortured, and killed. So, no. I haven't figured it out. Why don't you just tell me what you're going on about? I don't have time for riddles and mysteries."

He kissed her again and she let out a whimper as he took her bottom lip between his teeth and glided his tongue along it. "You're playing the victim again, half-blood. You know I don't like when you do that," he whispered.

Something about his kiss overwhelmed her with emotion. She could feel the hardness between his legs as it pressed against her pelvis. To make matters worse, as he cupped her buttocks, she felt her own arousal. Why hadn't she grown hot with desire when Lawson kissed her? Why didn't her most secret spot warm and throb when he touched her?

Lawson. This suddenly felt wrong. Very wrong.

"Stop, Rickard. I loved Lawson. You know that," she said, despite her desperation for him to continue his seduction.

He pulled back. The look of anger and hurt on his face shocked her. When he let her go, she fell to the floor with a thud.

Rickard turned his back on her.

Rowen came to her feet and rubbed her bum where she'd fallen. No words formed on her lips as she watched him pace the shop. The heat from his fury was palpable, and she stepped as far away from him as possible.

"Rickard?"

He spun around and pointed a finger at her face. His eyes narrowed. "Prince Rickard to you." He walked toward her, his boots loud on the wooden floor. "I'm only going to tell you this once, and I can only hope it's enough to get it through your thick skull. You are not a victim, Rowen. You are a key. Do not get caught. Get...lost."

With that, he opened the door, letting in a breeze that was cool and thick with the scent of a coming storm. He paused in the doorway and sighed. He took one look back at her. "Don't let all of my hard work go to waste, Rowen," he said, and left the shop.

Alone, and confused, Rowen rubbed her face. What was happening? What did he mean she was a key?

The cartwright came from the back room, chewing a piece of sugar cane. He was a tall, lanky man that looked to be in his sixties, with a bald head covered with white fuzz. "What'll it be, miss?"

Rowen stood there and shrugged, barely hearing his question as her mind raced with several of her own. She'd forgotten what she'd come for, where she was going, and what she would do next.

She felt cold and alone, and the effects of Rickard's touch, kiss, and words left her more lost than ever.

The day she'd met Prince Rickard had been in Princess Noemie's private quarters. It was her first day in the palace as a lady-in-waiting to the princess and she could barely keep her heart from beating out of her chest. This was the first step in executing the duke's plan to secure a spot as mistress to the crown prince of Withrae.

Nervous, frightened, and exhausted from the long journey from Harrow, Rowen watched him enter the room from her place in line with the other ladies-in-waiting. The first thing he'd done was to look them over as if they'd been brought there for him. Princess Noemie lounged on her chaise, sipping wine, a half-smirk on her lips as her brother walked down the line, examining them like cattle.

He joked about some of the girl's, right in front of their faces, and Rowen instantly knew she was not going to like him. Nonetheless, the others all batted their eyelashes and smiled at him.

Perhaps that was what made Rowen stand apart. She forgot to wear a smile, and so, he singled her out and stood before her.

"What's wrong with this one?" Rickard asked Noemie.

"There's nothing wrong with me, Prince Rickard," Rowen said, with a curtsy.

The other girls all turned to look at her.

He rubbed his chin and grinned. Something about his green eyes always enchanted her, but she fought it even then.

"Why such a serious face? Aren't you thankful to be here with the others?"

Princess Noemie sat up and came to her feet. "She's fine, Rickard. This is the half-blood from Harrow. Her mother is the Duchess. You know of her. She used to be mother's lady-in-waiting."

Realization filled his eyes and he nodded. "I see. The half-blood. This should be interesting," he said, tilting her chin to get a better look at her face.

It was with that first touch that Rowen knew she should stay as far away from Rickard as possible. With that touch, a tingling sensation ran along her skin, her body yearned for him, and her heart begged for him. From the look in his eye and how he snatched his hand back...he felt it too.

Dangerous.

Rowen did not come for the young prince. She came for the heir. And so, she built a brick wall around her heart and resisted him at every turn. But, one thing remained.

Rickard never gave up.

Still, as she remembered those days and walked from the cartwright's shop back to the inn, she always knew there was something powerful about Rickard's touch.

CHAPTER 8

A STORM STARTED TO BREW as Elian and Siddhe had their breakfast at a little circular table under the window in their room. He didn't mind the coming storm. He welcomed it. The smell alone reminded him of better days at sea. He should be grateful that he still had his life. A beautiful woman sat across from him in nothing but a shirt, her mahogany hair braided over one shoulder. If only he could be content to live like this.

Soon, they'd leave their comfortable room and set off into the world again. There were many roads to travel, yet Elian was only interested in one. A stinging pain in his chest reminded him that he was running out of time.

Chunks of fresh cheese, bread, and roasted ham were devoured as he and Siddhe discussed what was next.

"Are you going to be okay if we go to Malcore?" Elian asked, examining the dryness of her skin. The further from sea they ventured, the weaker Siddhe became.

"I'll be fine. I've never let you down before," Siddhe reminded him as she rubbed her bread on her plate, sopping up the grease and juices from the ham.

"Right. If you're certain, we can go. I just need to figure out where to go once we are there. That damned girl is the key to finding out the next clue."

Rolling her eyes, Siddhe chewed and swallowed her last bit of bread. "Forget the girl. She was a snobbish brat, and we don't need her. We never did."

"She was my daughter," Elian said, meeting her eyes. That meant something to him. His blood ran through her veins.

"No, she wasn't. She was a trouble. Nothing more. Nothing less."

Of course, Siddhe didn't like Rowen. She was a reminder that Elian had once loved another. Perhaps she was right. Rowen was trouble. But, he needed her.

He sat back in his chair as Siddhe came to her feet and walked around the table to stand behind him. She rubbed his shoulders and leaned down to kiss his right earlobe.

"We'll make it work, Elian. We always have, haven't we?"

Elian patted her hand and nodded. "We have."

"Once we find the Red Dragon, all of our dreams will come true."

She was naïve to think it, but he didn't contest her. Instead, he pulled her around and into his lap. She wrapped her slender legs around his waist and the back of the chair and took his face into her hands.

A deep kiss woke his manhood even though they'd made love just moments ago. Her tongue tasted sweet and her full lips were soft as the plushest pillows. She opened his shirt and ran her warm hand across his chest. He imagined bending her over the table, her hair wrapped around his fist as he parted her legs and—

A knock came to the door, interrupting his fantasy. Elian blew a breath through pursed lips. He knew immediately who it was.

Siddhe pulled back with a growl. "Can that boy go an hour without bothering us?"

"Come in, Gavin," Elian called.

Gavin walked in, eating a banana. "Morning, Captain," he said, with a mouth full. "Siddhe."

Siddhe left Elian's lap and placed her hands on her hips. "What is it? Can't you do anything on your own?"

"I can," he said. He took one look at Elian and Siddhe's compromising position and a mischievous grin lifted the corners of his mouth. "But, pestering you two is so much more fun."

Elian rolled his eyes and buttoned his shirt. His fantasy could wait. "Since you have so much time on your hands, how about you go to the village livery and get us three horses?"

"Well, I was going to visit the innkeeper's daughter...but, I guess I can do that, too," Gavin said.

"Horses? I'd rather walk or ride in a carriage," Siddhe said, frowning. "Tried it once, and my thighs ached for days."

"You'll be fine, Siddhe. We'll even get you a saddle," Elian said as he stood. He handed Gavin a few coins from his coin purse. "Buy them, and get them ready. I want to leave here before noon."

Gavin accepted the money and nodded. "I'm on it. Anything else? Maybe a...straight blade for that forest growing on your chin."

The glare Elian sent to Gavin shut him up, but he could tell he fought a smirk. There was something odd about the young man. It was as if he didn't truly fear him like others. He couldn't put his finger on it, and instead exhaled.

"No, just be quick about it, and keep your mouth shut to any nosy villagers," Elian warned.

"Right," Gavin said. "I'll let you two get back to...whatever it was you were doing." He winked at Siddhe and slipped out into the hallway.

Elian pressed the door shut and closed his eyes. "That boy is going to make me snap his neck one day."

"No, you won't. He's too much like you."

He raised a brow, and looked over his shoulder. "He is not."

She shrugged. "I'm just saying, he's snarky, crass, and knows he's attractive. Just like someone I know."

"You think he's attractive?" Elian raised a brow and turned to her as she pulled on a pair of pants.

Such a shame. He still had hopes of taking her on the table. "What of it?"

He grunted and went to the window, cracking it open for fresh air. He rubbed his beard, which thickened with each day. Maybe he should shave before they left.

"Hurry up, Perdan! I'd like to settle in before the storm," a female voice shouted from outside.

Elian froze. He knew that voice. Once he leaned out of the window and saw the covered cart and the woman and young man unloading chests onto the ground.

She must have sensed him, for she shot a look his way. The color drained from her face.

Feyda Barnick.

The woman who sold him the treasure map.

CHAPTER 9

ELIAN STRODE UP TO FEYDA, crossing the inn's small courtyard, and clasped his hands before him. There was a knowing smile on his face. This was a welcome surprise for him, but it was clear that she was uncomfortable by the way she shifted her weight from one foot to the other. She whispered something to Perdan, and the young man nodded and turned away to continue what he was doing. Elian found it interesting that Perdan had taken out two chests from the back of the cart, only to put them back inside.

With a forced smile, she greeted him. Her usual rosy-red cheeks had paled at the initial sight of him. He knew how people feared him, but suspected there was more going on inside her head.

"Captain Elian Westin," she said, with a nod. "What's an old fraud like you doing this far inland? Encounter a bit of trouble, aye?"

Elian chuckled. He'd always admired Feyda's spunk. He had planned on killing her after she sold him the map, but the woman hexed him with one of her spells before he could execute his plan.

"No. I'm doing better than ever. What's a bitter old hag like you doing this far from high society? Isn't that your new clientele since I paid you a fortune for that map?"

"Of course. We're living quite the lavish life. Thanks to you," she said.

Perdan kept his distance and continued unloading their cart.

Thunder cracked above them, lighting the gray sky with flashes of color. Elian glanced up, breathing in its scent.

"Well, isn't that just lovely," he said. "I've never met a luckier pair than the two of you."

"That's why you hired us to find the map of the Red Dragon, isn't it?"

Elian's smile faded. His eye twitched. "What are you doing here, Feyda?"

The seriousness of his voice did not go unnoticed. She swallowed.

"There is a private sale of antiquities in Kabrick's capital. Ancient scrolls, runes, and maybe even a few soul crystals to add to my collection. You know I can't miss such an outstanding opportunity to get my hands on such things."

Rubbing his chin, Elian nodded. "Right. Makes sense to me."

She was lying. That much was certain. He could tell from the way her heart beat sped. He could hear it, even over another crack of thunder followed by lightning.

"And, what about you, Captain Westin? We've heard rumors of Dragons, and ships being burned...and your supposed death. Yet, here you stand," she said, opening her arms before him. "In the flesh."

Elian shrugged. "Rumors are funny that way. Never believe what you hear in taverns, miss."

"So, what are you doing here?"

"I'm on holiday."

"Holiday?" she repeated, lifting a brow.

"That's right. To the countryside."

"Sure, you are," Feyda said.

It was clear that neither believed each other, but they didn't come out and say it. It was a dance of pleasantries, and they were both skilled at it.

For a moment, he wondered if Feyda was in search for the Red Dragon as well. Then, he realized that it was impossible. The map was blank when she sold it to him. There was no way she could follow a blank map without a prophet from his line in tow. He respected her skill too much to press her any further. She'd risked more than her reputation retrieving his ancestral inheritance. After his mother was killed, and he was sent away, he thought he'd never find their prized artifacts and heirlooms.

No, this woman was more than an old hag.

She was one of the most powerful sorceresses he'd ever met, and she hid that fact well.

Clever. That's what she was.

"Well," Feyda said. "Unless you want to buy something, we'd better be getting inside. This old hag can't stand to get soaked through by the nasty storm that's brewing. I say there might be a bit of flooding by day's end."

"Do you? That means I have all day to pester you."

Her smile was unexpected. "You sure you want to do that, Captain? You may be able to steal souls and all, but I can still twist your bones with the flick of a hand."

Elian rubbed his hands together, recalling the pain she'd caused, and how it took days to subside.

Without removing her gaze from his, she spoke to her son. "Perdan. We best be getting inside now."

"Coming," Perdan said, still avoiding a direct look at Elian. He carried two chests stacked on top of one another and headed to the stairs that led up to the second level.

Elian watched them leave. He didn't state his suspicions, but he knew they were up to something. He looked up as heavy ran started to fall. It poured onto his face as he closed his eyes.

He'd find out what she was up to. Something told him his life depended on it.

"Captain," Gavin called, running from around the corner of the inn, soaked and with a ghostly look on his face.

Elian blinked through the rain. "What is it?"

Gavin wiped wet hair from his eyes and stood before him, out of breath. "I heard her," he said.

"Who?"

"Rowen, sir. I am certain of it."

Rowen. That got his attention. Elian grabbed Gavin by his shoulders. His eyes burned with fury and hope. "Where?

Gavin looked down at Elian's hands on him.

"Tell me!" Elian shook him.

"I heard her voice when I was in town. I was heading from the livery when I passed the cartwright shop and heard her."

"Did you see her?"

"No," Gavin said, shaking his head. "Can you let go of me?"

Elian let go, pushing him back against the hall wall made of stone that enclosed the inn. "Take me to her."

"But, she's not there anymore. I went to look for her in one of the shops, and by the time I got inside, she was gone. I didn't see her, but I know that voice. I'll never forget it."

Elian's eye twitched. Could it be? Feyda and Perdan were in town, with ambiguous motives. The way that young man couldn't even look at him was one warning. The way Feyda's heart raced when she saw him was another. There were just too many coincidences for this all to be chance. If Rowen was truly here, all his worries would be put to rest.

Cota's words came to him.

The map will lead you to your heart's desire. Your heart's desire will be the death of you. Unless you learn to desire differently.

He didn't know what she meant by that. All he knew was that Rowen had his map, and his map was life or death.

He looked to the second floor of the inn as thunder cracked across the sky, seemingly shaking the ground with its force.

"I hear you," he whispered to the storm.

Perhaps fate was on his side after all.

CHAPTER 10

WHEN ROWEN APPROACHED THE INN, Feyda was there waiting for her. Rain fell in all directions, with intense winds that threatened to pick Rowen up and carry her away. She threw a shawl over Rowen's head, put a finger to her mouth to quiet her protests, and led her away from the inn and through the back roads of town to their cart.

Perdan sat in the front seat, reigns in hands, and a pale color to his cheeks.

"What's happening?" Rowen asked. She held tight to the sack of frost-weed Feyda had her purchase as more heavy winds blew at them.

"Just get inside," Feyda said, holding the cart's back door open to let her in. "We don't have much time. Hand me the frost-weed."

Rowen sat down inside the cart and handed Feyda the sack.

Feyda dumped its contents into her hands. She closed her fingers over it and made a fist which she held out at arm's length. Her eyes shut and her hand began to glow.

Rowen watched carefully, leaning over for a better look as Feyda blew onto it and whispered words in a foreign language. Then, she threw her hands up, and blew white dust into the air and onto the cart's canvas cover. The cart shook, and without delay, Feyda pulled herself up and into the cart.

"Go, Perdan."

The cart rolled down the road and away from Billingsport as a storm raged above. Rowen pulled off her soaking wet cloak and shivered at the chill seeped into her bones.

Feyda noticed and wrapped her in a fur blanket she'd pulled out of one of the chests.

The fur felt nice against her skin, but the sound of thunder and lightning worried her that they might not make it much longer during the storm "What's happening, Feyda? Why are we leaving?"

"I think it's time we talk," Feyda said, settling beside Rowen on the cushion that lined the floor and wall. She took Rowen's hands in her own.

Rowen tensed as Feyda traced the lines of the palm of her hands. "What are you doing?"

"I know you're a sorceress," Feyda admitted. She sighed and shook her head. "I knew from the moment I laid eyes on you. And, I also knew that you were more powerful than any other I've ever seen. I just don't think you know it. Yet."

"I don't know what you're talking about." Rowen took her hands away and pulled the blanket tight around her body. She shook from the cold, but worked at keeping her face unreadable. No good could come from Feyda knowing what she could do.

"Stop pretending, Ro. You can't hide such a gift from me. I've lived amongst sorceresses and sorcerers all my life. I know when someone is gifted, and love...your gift could destroy our world if not tamed."

"You're crazy. I already told you who I was. You think I'd be your maid if I had special abilities to fall back on?"

"I do," Feyda said. "Since you're a fugitive sentenced for killing the crown prince of Withrae."

All color drained from Rowen's face. It was as if she'd been splashed with a cold bucket of water. Her fears were coming to fruition.

Rowen weighed her options, calculated them, and made a decision.

She sprung to her feet and raced to the cart's door. A forceful push of the door and she prepared to jump onto the dark, wet road behind them. Looking at the forest on either end and the way the trees swayed and blew with the wind, she second-guessed herself.

Feyda caught her by the arm, and Rowen spun on her, grabbing her by the neck.

Energy and power surged from the deepest depths of her being, and out of her fingers. A shiver ran up her spine as she gripped the power and held tight.

"Take your hands off of me, and forget you ever met me," Rowen commanded through clenched teeth.

Feyda's eyes opened, and then she chuckled. First, it started soft. Then, her shoulders began to shake with laughter as she covered her mouth. Tears came to Feyda's eyes and she pried Rowen's hand from her neck.

"Now, I see," she said in between laughs. She clapped her hands. "We have a temptress on our hands. I knew it had to be something mental."

Rowen gasped, snatching her hand away. Not again. Did she lose her power, somehow? How could it not work on Gavin and Feyda?

Feyda howled with laughter and slapped her thighs as she settled back onto the ground. "Sit down, Ro. You're not going anywhere."

She lifted a hand and the door slammed shut. The lock fell into place from the outside with a metallic clang.

Frozen in terror, Rowen stood there, expecting the worse.

"I know you're wondering why your power didn't work just now. There's nothing wrong with you. Quite the opposite. I could feel your power, and how strong it is. I could also feel that there is more hidden within. It's like a river—held back by a dam—desperate to be freed for its full force. I must say, I can't wait to teach you to master it." Feyda looked to her. "Sit."

Rowen did as she was told, but kept her distance. She sat with her back pressed to the cart's door. "Why didn't it work?" Rowen asked.

"You can't tempt a sorceress or sorcerer, Rowen. That's just how it is. Our inner power combats yours."

Realization hit her.

Gavin was a sorcerer.

It all made sense. But, she wondered if he knew, or if he was just as good of an actor as she was.

"But, don't worry. There aren't many of us left in this world. Your power will work more times than not. I'll teach you what you need to know about your gift."

That was something Rowen had never heard before. No one had ever offered to help her—to teach her how to use her powers. Growing up, she kept it to herself. Not even her mother was aware of the strange urges Rowen had, and the struggle she suffered to control it. In the past, her usage of it had only been in times of desperation. Her shoulders slumped as she thought of those times, and how she'd just tried to use it on a woman who only wanted to help her.

"I'm sorry," Rowen said in a soft voice. She rubbed her arms and pulled her legs into her chest. As she wrapped her arms around her legs, she rested her head on her knees and shoved the painful memories as far back into her mind as possible.

"No one is blaming you, Ro. I understand. You've been reacting to everything purely on instinct. It's time for a different strategy."

"You're right. I didn't mean to try my power on you. I was frightened and needed to get away."

Feyda leaned forward, her brows raised. "Haven't you been listening? I knew who and what you were when I first saw you. If I wanted to turn you back in to the Dragons, I would have done it days ago. I'm sure there's a pretty penny to be made, but that's not what I'm looking for."

"What are you looking for," Rowen asked.

Feyda pointed to Rowen's chest and flicked her finger up, revealing the map and carrying it through the air toward her.

Rowen stood and reached for it, but Feyda was too fast. Before she could blink a second time, the map was in Feyda's hands.

Feyda snickered and opened it. Her eyes widened as she looked it over, and traced the path with her finger. "I want what everyone seems to be after these days."

"What is that?"

"The infamous Red Dragon, of course."

Later that night, Perdan and Feyda switched spots so that they could ride through the night. He and Rowen lay on the loft bed as the cart gently rolled along the dirt path. An occasional rock or bump made them rock, but the quiet hum of the wheels and the horse's steady gait was relaxing.

Rowen still couldn't sleep. There were too many things on her mind, and enough unanswered questions to keep her awake for days. She rolled over to Perdan who rested on his back with an arm under his head.

"Are you asleep?"

He opened his eyes and looked to her. "Not yet. What's wrong?"

She shook her head. "Nothing. Just wishing I were in my bed back at home. Well, only if my stepfather wasn't there. It would be perfect without him."

Perdan faced her, turning on his side. "Tell me about him. Is that who sent you to the palace?"

She exhaled. It was odd knowing that Perdan and Feyda had known her secret all along. She shouldn't have been surprised. News of the half-blood who killed the crown prince would have travelled faster than most throughout the realm. There was no escaping her past.

"Yes," she said. "He is a horrible man. Not only did he waste his money, but my mother's as well. Then, he expected me to help him rebuild his fortune."

"How?"

She hated the answer. It made her sound like a bad person. But, sometimes she wondered if that were true.

"By seducing Prince Lawson," she said. "But, I loved him, Perdan. I didn't expect that to happen. He was just too perfect not to love."

"I saw him once. He was quite handsome," Perdan said, nodding.

Rowen narrowed her eyes at him

"Perdan," she said. "I saw you kiss a man."

He shrugged. "What of it?"

She wasn't sure what she meant by bringing it up, but it had sat on her mind since it happened. "Well, I've heard of such things. I didn't believe they were true. I'd never seen anything like that before."

He cracked a grin. "I like beautiful things, Ro. Beautiful art. Beautiful men. Beautiful women."

"But, how?"

He raised a brow. "Oh, I see. You've fallen for me haven't you, Ro?"

Her cheeks flushed. "Nonsense."

"I understand. I'm charming and handsome. But, don't take offense. You're beautiful...but you're also too pale and thin for me. Besides, it's sinful for two blonds to be together."

Rowen laughed. Leave it to Perdan to cheer her up with his jests. "You're ridiculous. You're more like a brother than a lover," she said, playfully pushing his shoulder .

"I know, Ro. Now, go to sleep. We have a long journey ahead of us."

Rowen turned away from him on her side. He wrapped an arm around her and snuggled into her back.

"Dream of the future, if you can. Where all will be well, and you will once again find love."

She nodded and let his words lead her to sleep.

CHAPTER 11

THE DAYS WERE LONG AS they travelled the narrow roads that led from Billingsport to Malcore. Rowen was tired of thunder and lightning. The storm hadn't stopped, but as they drew closer to the Wasteland, the rain slowed to little more than a sprinkle, and then stopped completely.

Rowen looked out the window to the dark skies. A breeze blew at her face and rustled the curtain as she leaned out for a better look. A mixture of purples, grays, and orange danced across the sky as bolts of lightning illuminated the clouds from behind.

"I'm starting to forget whether its day or night," she said to Perdan who sat next to her.

What she'd give for a bowl of hot stew and a warm bed with thick blankets and plush pillows. Those were distant memories. Her mind drifted to Prince Rickard. It did that often after her last encounter with him. She didn't tell Feyda or Perdan, but kept it to herself and closed her eyes to relive his kiss. She'd wake up in a sweat after dreams of him and his seductive voice. They'd always start with passionate kisses and would morph into him pulling her by her hair to the gallows.

Best to forget him and his riddles.

"It's about noon," Perdan said, sipping water from a flask. He read from an ancient text sprawled across the floor of the cart.

"It's been three days since we've passed an inn. I would love a bath. A proper one with perfumes, oils, and hot stones."

"Why don't you sit down and make us some lunch? I can pour some of the rain water we collected over you later. Doesn't that sound nice?"

She slumped back inside the cart and combed through her hair with her fingers. "Make it yourself. There's only dried meat and cheese," she said. "And there isn't much of that left."

"Sounds lovely," he said, looking to her. "I'll take some of the cheese, with a smidge of mom's jam."

She still owned them her life, and Perdan had driven them with very little breaks for days on end. It was the least she could do. She crawled over to the far end of the cart where they kept their food and supplies in a drawer that pulled out from the small loft bed. Though Feyda repaired the canvas cover, it still leaked in some places, and they collected the water in a small bucket for washing their dishes. She cut some of the hard, white cheese and ladled a scoop of Feyda's peach and raisin jam beside it. She took a bite of the cheese and returned to Perdan.

"Thank you." Perdan yawned and accepted the small wooden bowl she'd prepared for him. "I might need a nap after this."

"Stay alert," Feyda shouted from the front where she directed the horses.

Rowen's eyes widened. "She really does hear everything."

"This lightning is getting closer. We may need to stop and do another enchantment on the cart before we get hit."

The horses squealed as a bolt of lightning struck a nearby pine tree. Bare of leaves, the tree caught on fire with flames reaching high into the sky.

"Calm down," Feyda shouted to the horses as they bucked and neighed with fear. "Shush now."

They stopped and Perdan opened the door. "I'll tend to them," he said, hopping down to the ground.

Rowen followed him. The smell of the air was odd. Something foul was in the air, but she couldn't place what it was. She looked around. Her hair blew into her face as stronger winds swept through the barren opening of a long valley between two red mountains.

"What is this place?"

Perdan glanced back at her as he ran to the horses. "We're deep in it, now, Ro. This is just the beginning of the Malcore Wastelands. Nothing lives past this point."

Her eyes rose as she looked at the mountains. They were as tall as those in Withrae, reaching high into the clouds with peaks vanishing into the sky.

Another crack of lightning shot into another tree behind Rowen and she was thrown backward by the force of the explosion. She fell to the ground and slid a few feet across the ground, scraping her arms and legs. Groaning, she pushed herself up to her elbows and tried to clear her vision. For a moment, she could hear nothing. Then, gradually, the sound of the horses going crazy and Perdan's shouting for her started to ring in her ears.

"Ro! Are you okay?"

Feyda ran to her and helped her to her feet. "Are you hurt?"

"I'm fine," Rowen said in between quick breaths.

"It's all catching fire!" Feyda shouted as the blaze from the trees started spreading.

Before they could react, they were encircled by a ring of fire with flames so intense that Rowen and the others started to sweat, smoke rose from the ground, and the horses went mad.

"I'm trying to hitch the horses so we can get out of here," Perdan shouted to them as he grabbed the reins of the horses and tried to keep them from running off.

A horse bucked and tore the reigns from Perdan's hands. "Can I get some help?"

Rowen ran to him. She placed her hands on the horse's neck and closed her eyes. She'd never used her power on an animal before, but gave it a try nonetheless.

"Calm down," she whispered. "Shh. Everything will be fine. Just stay still."

"Ro!" Feyda yelled to her. "What in blazes are you doing? Don't Tempt the bloody horse! Tempt the fire!"

She shot a look of bewilderment to the older woman. Tempt the fire? "What? I can't do that."

Feyda gathered her skirts and marched over to her. She narrowed her eyes. "But, you can. Give it a try. What harm is there in trying?"

She opened her mouth to protest, but snapped it shut and closed her eyes. *Feyda has lost her mind.* There was no use arguing with her. She opened her eyes and stepped away from the horses. "Fine. I'll give it a try."

"You can do it. Find the line of energy and bend it to your will. Anything can be Tempted. Trust me."

With a snort, Rowen closed her eyes and held out her hands. Trust was a word that didn't sit well with her.

She breathed in and exhaled, calming her heart and breathing so that she could devote her energy to focusing. Her hands tingled as her power searched for a target. Inside her mind, she could see it whipping out from her fingers without any guidance.

"To the fire," she whispered, her brows knitting together as she tried to control the power. It pulled her forward and yanked her to the fire. Rowen gasped and opened her eyes. What she saw before her took her breath away.

"You're doing it, Ro! Keep it going. Bend the fire away from the cart and horses."

Her eyes widened as the flames wavered and pulled in her direction. She could see her power, like a mist of green grabbing it. "And, do what with it?"

"Just move it out of our way so we can get out of here," Feyda said, waving toward the flames. "Hurry, Ro."

Rowen pulled the blaze further away, opening a small pathway, but not big enough for the cart to fit through. Her forehead beaded with sweat and she felt her breaths grow shallow. It took a great deal of energy to manipulate the fire and her arms started to weaken.

A tree fell in front of the horses and the flames licked and ran along the cart.

"Grab what you can from the cart," Perdan shouted.

Feyda placed her hands to her cheeks as she looked at their cart in flames. "No," she said.

She and Rowen ran and grabbed what they could before the flames took over and consumed everything. With the last of their water, a few of Feyda's potions and what was left of their meager remnants of food, they were utterly lost. The horses fled, and Rowen and the other ran from the cart just in time as the entire thing burst into flames.

"Forgot to grab the damned Dragon's breath," Feyda grumbled as they watched the horses run in the other direction.

Away from the flames, they all stood there watching the disaster before them.

"Well, at least we're alive," Perdan said, catching his breath.

Feyda huffed. "Not for long. We're in the Wastelands. If we don't die from starvation or thirst, the elements will certainly take a stab at us."

"We do still have the map," Perdan said.

"And no idea where it leads after this valley," Feyda pointed out.

"We have to find shelter," Rowen said. Her survival instinct spoke before she truly had a plan. "Come, let's go find somewhere to rest and think of a plan."

Feyda and Perdan both looked at her and silently nodded.

It was odd having Rowen lead the way. As they walked from the burning cart, she rubbed her hands together. She now knew of a new power, one she never imagined. She just didn't know what good it would do them out there in the barren wilderness of the Wildlands.

She looked to the sky as lightning cracked again.

Where was her good friend, Luck now?

CHAPTER 12

NIGHT BEGAN TO SHIFT THE colors of the sky from blue to orange and purple as the sun retired and the clouds hid it away.

Prince Rickard walked the narrow streets of Lindenhold, a port on the southern tip of Withrae. He was cloaked and in clothing a commoner would wear. He kept his head down as he passed a few Withraen Navy soldiers gathering supplies for their trek back home. He didn't need to get recognized. Not before his plan was fully executed.

No one paid him any mind, and he slipped away from the port crowds and into the small island town. Sailors and pirates escaped into taverns and brothels, and the people of Lindenhold retired to their homes after a long day of work on the docks and in the mines not too far from the harbor.

No one knew him around here, and that worked in his favor.

His destination awaited in a dark corner, where vines covered most of the stone walls, almost hiding it. He knocked on the door.

A small girl opened it, slightly, and peeked at him with big eyes. A buck-toothed grin came to her lips. "Prince Rickard."

He stepped inside when she opened the door for him. "Call me Rick, Cota. I don't need the entire town knowing I was here."

"Course, sir. Won't happen again," she said, attempting a curtsy.

Rickard exhaled. "Just close the door and keep it down."

She closed the door and almost giddily clapped her hands and motioned for him to take a seat. "I woulda' known you were comin' this way...Rick, I woulda' cleaned up a bit."

He sat in one of the chairs at the small table pressed against the whitewashed wall. He looked around. She'd made some improvements to the home she shared with her brother, Trenneth.

"Like it?" Cota asked, sitting on the rug on the center of the floor at his feet. "Trenneth painted the walls and patched up all of the holes in the ceiling. Quite cozy now, aye?"

"Yes," Rickard said. "Cozy. Tell me about Captain Elian Westin. He came here not too long ago. What did you two talk about?"

Cota shrugged. "Same stuff, really. The map. The Red Dragon. Wish he'd come more often. Funds are gettin' low."

She was being vague for a reason. Rickard rolled his eyes and pulled out a purse of gold coins. "That should last you a few years."

Her eyes grew larger as she took the purse from his hands and looked inside. Funny how quickly she started spilling everything she knew.

"I told 'em about the map and how its gonna kill 'em."

"What do you mean it's going to kill him?"

She shrugged. "Don't know for certain. The dark souls didn't tell me."

Rickard leaned forward. "Did you tell him anything about the half-blood dragon?"

Cota tilted her head. Her silence worried him.

If she told him the secrets of the half-blood dragon prophecy, it could ruin everything. Perhaps he should keep what he knew to himself and not give away any clues. The last thing he needed was Cota selling information back to Elian. Or worse, his father, King Thorne. If she'd seen anything that linked the map, the Red Dragon, and the half-blood dragon he needed to know.

It was worth the risk. What he had planned was greater than anything and anyone involved. It was enough to change the world.

She blinked up at him, suspiciously quiet.

At the very least, he could pay her brother, Trenneth extra to keep an eye on her and make sure she kept her mouth shut.

"Did you see anything about the half-blood dragon in your visions?"

Cota tilted her head, smiling. She nodded. "Aye. I saw her. She was beautiful."

Yes, she was.

"What else did you see?"

Cota picked at a loose string on her apron. "Can't say. Was too dark. Was a lot of blood."

That made him sit up. "Whose blood?"

"Not hers," she said. "'Twas everyone elses."

His brows knitted together. "What do you mean?"

"I don't know. I think she killed everyone."

That was unsettling. Rickard sat back in his chair and scratched his head. There must be a new prophecy he hadn't studied. Rowen must be growing stronger.

"Anything else?"

She shook her head. "Like I said. 'Twas dark. The dark soul didn't want me to see too much. Was not my business."

He stood and headed for the door. "I can trust you to keep this meeting and what I told you a secret, can't I?"

She grinned and held up the coin purse. "I'll do whatever you ask...Rick."

"Good." He left her home, pulling his cloak's hood back over his head. As he left the alley Cota lived on, he tried to make sense of the pieces of prophecy Cota had seen. He needed more information in order to execute his plan. There was no room for error.

Not when he planned to kill his father and take over the Withraen Throne.

CHAPTER 13

THE GATEKEEPER STOOD ON A platform at the bottom of a tall black tower, dressed in a long blue robe embroidered with glittering silver threads that made up symbols of their duties. Flying was exhausting, and he hadn't much time. If he wanted to return home and set back out on his mission, Rickard would need a quick solution.

His visit with Cota had been enlightening. Now, he needed to work another part of his plan.

One that was more dangerous.

Armed with a few coins, he approached the older woman with long black hair. Silver strands stood out from the others and a yellow aura encircled her body. She held a golden rod that was over a foot taller than her in one hand and a book bound with flesh in the other. This was one of the only forms of the old magic to still be allowed in their society, and for good reason. Rickard couldn't even imagine what terrible fate would befall them if they attempted to execute a Gatekeeper.

Her white eyes lowered to him as he stopped and fished the coins out of his pocket. He placed them in the hands of a small boy with long, dark hair who sat on the ground before her, his legs crisscrossed. His eyes were white just like the Gatekeepers.

As her apprentice, they'd never return to their normal color for as long as he lived. The symbol of their class was also burned into his forehead, a circle with a line cutting through the middle and up the length of his forehead, and down to the tip of his chin.

He counted them and looked up with a smile. "Please proceed to the Gatekeeper."

Rickard took off his cloak's hood and knelt before the Gatekeeper.

"Is your soul clean?"

He nodded. "It is."

A Gatekeeper could not transport anyone who had recently committed a crime against the flesh. Murderers. Rapists. Anyone who had committed an evil such as those would be turned to dust if they attempted a Port after a crime. It was just one way the realm kept crime in order. It wasn't perfect, but it served its purpose.

Rickard was lucky. He hadn't killed anyone in weeks.

"Where would you like to go? I can send you as far as Harlsburg."

"Central Withrae," he answered.

He keep his head down, and resisted one last look at her crystalline white eyes. She tapped his head with the end of her golden rod, and within seconds, his body began to go translucent as a mist rose from the ground and took him away.

The ride was quick, and painless. But, when he opened his eyes to the bright sun of Withrae, he was a bit wobbly on his feet. He inhaled and looked around from the top of the Withraen Gatekeeper's Tower. White, stone steps led down to the paved streets of his kingdom. Instead of walking down them, he shifted and flew into the horizon, toward the grand castle that stood far away, just before the mountains his ancestors once ruled.

The Withraen Castle was quieter than it had once been. Only weeks ago, the halls had been cheerier, with beautiful ladies and regal lords lingering each season to gain favor in the king's court. A somber mood had taken over, and Rickard did not approve.

Lawson was dead, but the living had to go on. Whoever killed him knew what they were doing, and how it would change things.

He'd mourned his brother's death in private. Locked in his room, he tried to forget the memories of their childhood together, even though most were marred by his older brother's torment of him. Once, there had been an innocent child within Lawson, one of love and compassion. That innocence had died long before he did.

The world thought Lawson was the golden child, their savior.

He scowled.

Nonsense.

As Rickard walked up the stairs to the throne room, he grimaced. Lawson was no savior, and would have made their father look like a saint if he'd had been allowed to become king of Withrae. All of Draconia and the human realms would have been shaken by his rule and thirst for power.

But, that was a secret the world was not ready to know.

He fixed his clothes. After the flight from the Gatekeeper's tower to the castle, he had bathed and changed into something more appropriate for the new heir of Withrae.

The throne room was quiet. At the back of the room were three large windows that stretched from floor to ceiling. They were open, in case the king wanted to stretch his wings and fly to the Keep where he spent most of his time studying the ancient texts and forgotten prophecies.

Today, he stood at the window in the center, his hands clasped behind his back.

"Rickard," he said in a deep voice that echoed off of the walls of the room. "Where have you been?"

Rickard strode across the room toward him, swallowing back a fleeting sense of fear. He freed his face of all emotion, something he'd learned from Rowen.

She was a remarkable woman, one who in such a short amount of time had reeled him in. Such a feat would have been thought impossible until she arrived.

With one look, and one touch, he knew.

She was made for him, and he was made for her.

She was an expert at hiding her true feelings, and he mimicked her to no avail.

One look from King Thorne, and he knew his face had paled.

The paling was quickly replaced with a crimson red when his father slapped him hard across the cheek.

Rickard tasted blood. His hands balled into fists, but instead of letting out the rage that boiled in his belly, he closed his eyes and took in a deep breath.

The king spoke in an even tone. There was no anger, or even a raise in his voice.

Always calm.

Collected.

Downright devilish.

"Where is the half-blood?"

Rickard wiped his mouth and looked at the blood that streaked his fingers. It took a moment for him to reign in his rage, but he swallowed it down and cleared his head. He could handle the abuse, for a while longer.

"I haven't found her," he said, lifting his gaze to his father's deep indigo eyes. "Yet."

King Thorne had white hair, cut short and a matching beard. It was a bright contrast to his leathery bronzed face. Rickard wasn't fair like his brother, and that was because he took more after their father. The similarities ended at the physical traits.

Thorne was strong, despite his age, and still the fire of a Dragon running through his veins.

He was nowhere near his deathbed. Rickard looked forward to changing that.

"I'm running out of patience. Find her, kill her, or bring her to me so I can see her hang. Do you understand?"

"Why? We both know she didn't kill Lawson."

"I didn't ask for your questions. You do as I say or you'll be turned to the mountains, where you can live out your days imprisoned with the other beggars and thieves," he said, tightening his jaw.

"Fine," Rickard said. "I've vowed to find her, and so I will. But, the kingdom will hate you for what you're doing...when they find out the truth."

Thorne smirked. It lifted the corner of his mouth, but his eyes narrowed and burned with hate as he looked at Rickard. "Let them. Soon, the world will know the true strength of the Thorne clan, and immortality will mute any opposition to my rule."

Rickard kept quiet.

As he focused on relaxing his fists and convincing himself not to punch his father in the face, he admitted that Thorne was right about one thing. Immortality would mute any opposition.

Just not for his rule.

CHAPTER 14

ROWEN CRINGED AS SHE TOOK a small bite of the gristly meat of a Wasteland scoottail. She wanted to spit it out, but the hunger from barely eating anything for two days made her think twice and continue chewing. Swallowing it down wasn't any easier. But, at least it quieted the nagging pain in her empty stomach. She closed her eyes and tore more of the tough meat with her teeth.

"I vow to never eat scoottail ever again," she said.

Feyda shrugged, rubbing her hands in front of the fire. "It's not that bad."

For such hot days, the nights of the Wastelands were frigid with winds that blew so forcefully that it was hard to keep a fire going. They depended on Rowen to keep the fire alive.

With her newfound power.

"No, its worse," she said, trying to ignore the foul flavor on her tongue. "Did you know these are considered delicacies to the Dragons of Withrae? They'd eat them in a thick spicy red sauce on a platter for special occasions in the palace. I doubt they'd ever tasted a real one. I can't see how anyone could stomach it."

Perdan took another rat-sized scoottail from the stick they had over the fire. He didn't seem to mind the taste or the texture and ate it all within seconds.

She watched him with her jaw hanging as he tossed the bones into the fire and rested on his back, his arms folded under his head.

"You can always hand me yours if you don't want it."

"Considering we have nothing else, I'll make do," she said to him.

They were without shelter, thirsty, and starving. There was no other choice if she wanted to survive.

The storms continued to light the sky with flashes of color and loud bangs that shook the valley. They never let up for a moment. Lightning and thunder flickered across dark skies. This was a forsaken place where no one should ever venture. Yet, there they were, hopeful to find a mysterious treasure.

Rowen had no idea what the Red Dragon could or would do. But, her last prophecy showed it to her. That must mean something. Even if she just needed to meet the dragon to prevent a fate worse than her own hanging, she knew deep down inside that she had to do it.

"This is a good time to practice, Ro," Feyda said, scooting closer to her. "The fire is dying. See if you can give it new life."

She nodded and popped the last piece of meat into her mouth. She rubbed the grease from her fingers onto her cracked lips.

"Grab the flames and feed it more energy."

The flames started to dwindle, barely licking the thin sticks they'd gathered during the day, and the brush they'd stuffed into the center. They needed that fire to burn stronger if they were going to survive another cold night, but Rowen didn't tell Feyda how each time she attempted this new skill it drained her. Not only did Feyda want her to keep the fire burning, but she had Rowen create thin lines of fire that chased the scoottails into Perden's traps.

Her power was keeping them alive.

Instead, she sucked in a breath and narrowed her eyes. Much better than she was the first time, she lifted one hand and twirled her finger. The flame jerked and flickered toward her. Embers flew into the air like fireflies.

"Good girl," Feyda whispered, squeezing Rowen's shoulder with joy. "You're doing it."

She raised her hand, and the flame followed, gaining height and power. Then, with a twist of her hand, she made the flame swirl and burst into a raging fire that lit up their surroundings.

Perdan sat up, his eyes widened. "That was new."

Smiling, Rowen nodded. "It was. It felt a little strange, but I like it. I can tell that I'm getting more powerful."

"Good job, Ro," Feyda said, rubbing her hands and face in front of the fire.

"Thank you. Maybe, once we are free from this valley, fed, and had our fill of fresh water and wine, you can teach me some more."

Feyda smiled back at her. "I'd like that. You're a fast learner." She glanced at Perdan. "Unlike someone I know."

"You can't be talking about me," Perdan said, and indignant look on his face. His cheeks had already began to sink in from malnutrition. Rowen hated what was happening to them.

"I am," Feyda said. "Took you two years to learn a simple Charm of Deep Sleep."

He scoffed. "That's because you had me practice on the pigs back in Reeds. Not the best of specimens."

Feyda chuckled and returned to warming her hands.

Drained, Rowen rolled onto her side, facing the fire. Though she could barely keep her eyes open, she took out the map and gave it one last look. They were so close to the last marked spot. One more day and they might find another clue that would lead them to the Red Dragon.

She folded the map and groaned at how tired she was.

"Get some sleep," Feyda said, rubbing Rowen's back. "We have much ground to cover tomorrow."

Nodding, Rowen drifted. There was one face she saw when her dreams took over.

Rickard's.

This time, her body tensed and her heart raced. This was not a dream. She tried to wake up, to sit up, but while her mind was awake, her body was paralyzed.

This was a prophecy.

Instead of panicking, Rowen controlled her breathing and focused on what the prophecy had to show her. This was her greatest power. One she didn't even tell Feyda and Perdan about.

Rickard took her by the hand. This time he wasn't leading her to the gallows. Instead, he lead her down a path of golden stone that cut through a lush rose garden. The green vines wrapped around white pillars and a wall of rose bushes rose higher than their heads. It was a sunny day, with a purple sky customary for a Withraen spring afternoon.

She followed him, and she was not afraid. Dragons flew above their heads, swirling like vultures. What were they waiting for?

"Are you paying attention?" Rickard asked. His voice was hollow and seemed to come from faraway even though he stopped and stood right in front of her. He was dressed in a fine black suit. His hair was pulled back in a ponytail, and his face was still clean-shaven. She could even smell the scent that had become so familiar to her that she would know if Rickard had been in a room long after he'd left.

"Ready for what?" she asked.

He held his finger to his lips and grinned. "Shh. I'll show you."

Together, they walked to the end of the golden road to a cliff. Rowen gasped as a red dragon flew up from the destruction below. She fell to her knees and gawked at the horrific scene. Dragons were blowing fire onto humans who ran in all directions screaming with their children in their arms.

"What is this?"

Rickard stood beside her, stroking her hair, but he didn't reply.

The screams grew so loud that she had to cover her ears with her hands.

Blood splattered on Rowen's face as the Red Dragon dropped Lawson's body on the ground before her.

She screamed at the sight of his face. Blood was caked around his mouth from the poison. His eyes were rolled back into his head, and his skin was a pale gray. This was not the Lawson she knew. She wished she could forget that image. It was a cruel sight to see.

Rickard leaned down and laughed, infuriating her.

"What is this?"

Her scream filled the valley as Rowen shot up from her dream-like state.

Her heart raced and her face was wet with sweat. Her vision cleared and what she saw made her blood run cold.

Captain Elian Westin knelt down before her, a wicked grin on his face.

Gavin and Siddhe stood on either side of her, and Feyda and Perdan were gagged and tied with ropes. Siddhe held a dagger in her hand and flashed its steel under the moonlight as she folded her arms across her chest and tapped it against her arm.

Rowen swallowed. The grins on their faces were almost more terrifying than the prophecy she'd just witnessed. Now, she wished that she hadn't made the fire bigger. It made them vulnerable and easily traced.

"What is this?" Elian repeated. His soft chuckle made the hairs on the back of her neck stand on end. "It's my lucky day."

CHAPTER 15

WHAT A SPLENDID TURN OF events. Elian glanced over his shoulder at his prisoners. Feyda, Perdan, and Rowen were bound and gagged next to the crackling fire. He and the others had trailed the trio for days, keeping their distance, buying their time. It seemed that patience did indeed pay off, and now he had his map, his daughter, and two fresh sorcerer souls to consume.

"What now?" Gavin asked in a whisper.

Siddhe lifted her dagger. "I can slice Rowen's hand off and we can carry it with us the rest of the journey to finding the Red Dragon," she said. "That way, we don't need to drag her along. I'll slit their throats and we can be on our way."

Gavin's eyes widened in horror. "Wait a minute. No one said anything about killing her."

"What do you care?" Siddhe asked.

He shrugged. "I don't," he muttered. "But, she's just a girl. A severed hand won't do us any good once the blood dries. Just get her to bleed on the map and let them go."

"We can collect her blood in a vial," Siddhe pointed out. "Easy."

Shaking his head, Gavin sighed. He clasped his hands in front of his face as he tried to reason with Siddhe. "No. It's not easy." He raised his brows. "What is wrong with you?"

Siddhe shrugged.

Elian weighed both of their plans. Siddhe was right. They didn't need to waste time dragging her along. But, he wasn't sure he could kill his own daughter. There was something there that hadn't been explored and he had a feeling he'd need her.

"Gavin's right," Elian said.

A smile came to Gavin's face. "I am?"

"We will take her with us," he said. "I'll kill and suck the souls out of Perdan and Feyda, and we'll be on our way."

"Good idea," Siddhe said.

Gavin's smile dropped. "It is not!"

"Shut up, Gavin," Elian said.

Gavin threw up his hands. "You two are lunatics."

Elian could already feel the surge of energy the souls of two sorcerers would give him. Energy was a resource he'd been low on for the past week.

"Captain," Gavin said, standing in front of him. He blocked Elian's view of the terrified prisoners.

"Move, Gavin. Or I will have to move you myself. Trust me, you won't like it if I have to do that."

"But, Captain, think about it. They obviously know about the Red Dragon. Right? Perhaps there is something we can learn from them. Say...like who they're working for, and what they had planned on doing with it once they'd found it. If you kill them, you have no idea who might come after us."

"How do you know Feyda isn't doing this on her own?"

"Come, now. Do you really believe that? No, I think she's an agent for someone with enough money and power that we don't want to anger them. Besides, do you think it's a coincidence that Rowen is with them?

Elian paused. He thought about what Gavin said. How could he be so blind? None of this was merely a coincidence. This was all someone's grand design. Now, he wondered who the Dragon was that rescued Rowen from his ship.

The crackling of the fire filled the silence as Elian weighed his options.

He refused to say it again, but Gavin was right.

"He's right," Siddhe said, and they both turned and looked at her as if she'd grown three heads. "What? Why are you looking at me like that?"

Siddhe just proved that miracles do happen.

He stroked his bead and strode over to Rowen. She looked up at him with terror in her big, gray eyes. Why did she have to have his eyes?

He pulled her up by her arm and took her away from the others. Once around the corner of the mountain, he removed her gag.

She opened her mouth and he clamped his hand over it.

"No use screaming. There isn't any food for miles, which means there isn't anyone looking for food. So, save your energy. No one is going to hear you."

He removed her hand and she licked her lips. "What do you want? You have your map. Let us go."

"I want to know why you were looking for the Red Dragon."

"Who says I was?" Rowen asked.

"Don't be cheeky with me. Tell me."

"I don't know what you're talking about. What is the Red Dragon? Why are you looking for it?"

Elian growled and yanked her closer. "That is none of your business. I am the one asking the questions. You're in no position to play this game."

"But, Father," she said, softly. "Tell me what you want me to say, and I'll say it."

He froze at her calling him father. He let her arm go and closed his mouth, swallowing a lump in his throat.

For a moment, he was taken aback and lost a bit of steam. Calmly, he closed his eyes and breathed in. "How did you meet Feyda?"

"I don't remember."

His anger resurfaced and he rubbed his temples. Was this what all parents had to deal with? If she wasn't his daughter, he'd have tortured her for answers. Never in all of his life did he even think of having children. Whenever he was with Nimah, it was all about her. She consumed his life and he was more than willing to give her more. If it wasn't for her family and their prejudices against humans, he'd still be with her.

And, he'd be looking at Rowen very differently. He might have even looked at her with love.

He took her by the arm and brought her back to the fire. He pulled the map from his pocket and held it in front of her face. "Tell me what I want to know. Or, I will let Siddhe here practice her knife skills on your friends."

Rowen looked to Feyda and Perdan who both had tears in their eyes and begged her from behind their gags.

"I don't know what you want! I don't know anything," Rowen insisted.

Elian forced her to her knees. He had enough of this.

"Bleed," he said. "Or they die."

CHAPTER 16

HARROW HALL SAT PROUD AND grim at the summit of a tall, grey mountain. Rickard curled his lip at the sight of it as he caught an updraft and allowed it to carry him higher, climbing in lazy spirals.

Two, small bronze scouting Dragons swooped down to confront him as he neared the courtyard designated for Dragon landings. They jerked their heads upward, giving the traditional territory challenge in Dragon body language. Rickard responded by tilting his body back, using the great sweeps of his wing for lift and balance as he bared his underbelly to them, signaling peaceful intentions.

They flew to his side and escorted him down to the cold flagstones of the courtyard. He closed his eyes and breathed through the familiar draining sensation of shifting back to human. The bronze dragons shifted back as well.

"I am come to speak with Her Grace," Rickard said.

"How are you to be announced?" one of the guards asked cautiously.

"As a friend...from Withrae."

The two guards exchanged frowns, and Rickard spoke up. "I assure you, I come in peace as a friend to the duchess, and since she is in disgrace with the duke, she can use all the friends she can get."

The other guard nodded, suspicion still written on his face. But, he went inside the keep and returned a few minutes later with a minor species of majordomo. The florid-faced, rotund little man seemed all too glad to have any kind of guest to tend to, even one who refused to give his name.

Rickard fought the urge to grumble as they climbed what felt like a ridiculous number of stairs. Really, couldn't Nimah have picked a receiving room that was a few floors lower? As if flying all the way up that gods-forsaken mountain wasn't enough, it was really beyond the pale to make guests trudge all the way up the tallest tower. But then, he thought sardonically, every princess needs her tower.

The fussy majordomo brought them to a set of double doors. Rickard noticed the paint on them was starting to peel, and the gilt was tarnished. He almost enjoyed the majordomo's confused announcement of an 'anonymous' visitor. The damask curtains were dusty, and the brocade cushions were threadbare. The same could be said for Nimah, Duchess of Harrow. She looked as if she had aged ten years in the three weeks that Rowen had been missing.

Nimah was too well-trained and well-bred to show any surprise or recognition upon seeing him. She simply dismissed all her attendants and sat still and quiet, waiting for him to make the opening play. He was not one to disappoint.

"Your Grace," he said, doing the pretty and bowing low enough to make a mockery of a prince bowing to a duchess.

To her credit, she played along and simply nodded at him. For a woman banished to the mountains in shame for the crimes of her daughter, she was remarkably dignified.

"Where is my daughter?"

Well, that was one way to cut to the chase. It seems that standing up to a husband was too much to ask for, but, being defiant in the face of a prince for the sake of her daughter was nothing at all.

"Indeed, that is the exact question I came all this distance to ask your Grace," he drawled, watching for the half-second her eyelids flickered.

"I swear upon the teeth of my ancestors that I do not know," Nimah said, the whites of her knuckles showing for the span of a heartbeat as she wrung the handkerchief in her grip. To make a vow upon the Dragon teeth of one's ancestor was serious enough that Rickard actually believed her.

The relief he felt was astounding. Rowen was on her way to being well and truly 'lost.' The Withraen royal prophecy actually stood a chance of being fulfilled.

Nimah looked nervous. He was familiar with that flitting gaze of a woman who was afraid of something...or someone. The someone wasn't hard to guess.

The duke.

He was sympathetic, but not patient.

"What do you know of the Withraen prophecy about the half-blood Dragon?"

Nimah's cheeks paled, but she shook her head, hesitant at first, and then with resolve.

Clever woman. If she did know the prophecy, she chose well to keep it a secret. Any mother would.

He chose silence as his weapon to force Nimah to speak further, knowing she wanted to deep down inside. If she was going to trust anyone, it should be the Dragon who could restore her favor with Withrae and save her from the duke— the Dragon who could truly protect her daughter.

Rickard examined her face and smiled. She knew more than she let on. She just wanted to know if he knew the answer.

Taking a gamble, he clasped his hands and exhaled. "If you knew anything about the prophecy, you'd know that it would take the half-blood and her father to find the Red Dragon. It cannot be done without the other. Do you see what I am saying, Nimah?"

Her bottom lip trembled. "But, I do not know if Elian knows she is his daughter." Tears came to her eyes. "He'll kill her before finding out."

"I won't let that happen."

Nimah raised a brow, a tear slipping from the corner of her right eye. "What can you do? You don't even know where she is."

"That's where you're wrong. I have a journal—one where I can communicate with all of my agents around the realm. Cota in Lindenhall. Cook...formerly of Elian's crew. And, a powerful sorceress named Feyda who I commissioned to take Rowen under her wing and guide her to the territory of the Red Dragon."

Nimah's eyes widened. "You do know where she is!"

Rickard nodded. "Of course. I wouldn't be good at what I do if I didn't. I just wanted to make sure no one else knew. The prophecy will not work if that is so."

She ran to him and wrapped her arms around his neck. "Thank you, your highness. I cannot thank you enough."

He patted her back and stepped away. "I already told you, Nimah. I've claimed Rowen."

She held tight to his hands, and when he looked at her, he gasped at how her eyes had changed to a silvery-white. Her voice also changed. It seemed to come from faraway.

"Save Rowen from her father. Do so, and you will save all of Draconia from doom."

Swallowing, Rickard waved his hand before Nimah's eyes. She'd essential spoken the words of the prophecy. But, it didn't seem like they truly came for her.

He backed away, toward the door.

"I will," he said. "I'll protect and love her until my dying breath."

CHAPTER 17

STARVATION IS A TERRIBLE WAY to die. As Rowen walked behind Elian and Siddhe, she realized that blistered feet were a close second. Her stomach screamed for sustenance, and her lips were chapped from dryness and thirst.

Her life had been in a steady decline since Lawson's death. A battle between fate's twisted sense of humor and her knack for being lucky had her torn about about what the world truly wanted from her. Her last prophecy still haunted her, but the agonizing death that seemed to lie ahead terrified her even more.

She didn't trust Elian, and so she resisted touching the map. What would happen if she did? She knew he'd kill her. If he no longer had any need for her power, there was no need to keep her alive.

Elian shared what little provisions he had, but barely. Soon, they would all starve and no one would make it to the Red Dragon. The dusty valley was little more than red rocks, dry orange dirt, and a sky of bright blue. They'd walked for days, and the storms had gradually stopped. Elian kept the map in his hand, and kept looking at it to make sure they were going the right way. Soon, he would need more of Rowen's blood to show him the exact location of the Red Dragon.

"What did your mother tell you about me," Elian said, falling into step beside Rowen. He looked at her with a sense of genuine curiosity, but she wasn't going to fall for his tricks.

"Too late for that, Elian," Rowen grumbled. "If you wanted to be a father, you wouldn't have left her behind to be tormented and forced into a marriage she didn't want."

Elian's eyes narrowed. "Forced? She was probably all too happy to join forces with another wealthy family. She married a Duke after all."

"And, he made me try to seduce the crown prince to replenish his squandered fortune," Rowen said, looking ahead. The bitterness of that truth tasted like salt on her tongue. "No one won in that arrangement but him."

"So, she's been miserable all of these years?"

Rowen nodded. "Thanks to you."

He kept quiet, then. She glanced at him and almost felt sorry.

Almost.

He'd made them suffer for something no one even seemed to understand. He seemed to be saddened by her words. Was it possible that he loved her mother? If he had, why would he leave her behind? She didn't speak her thoughts. If he felt badly, he deserved it.

"Rowen," he said, stopping to look at the map. He looked up at the mountains and his brows furrowed. "I need you to touch the map and make it tell us where to go next."

She shook her head. "I can't. The new power I have is too unstable. I'll ruin it and we'll all be stranded out here."

"It's true," Feyda said. "Rowen's power needs time and practice. She'll burn it up. Mark my words."

"Nonsense," Elian said. "What is this power you speak of?"

"She can manipulate fire," Perdan spoke up after days of quiet. Everyone looked to him. "I've seen her do it."

"She just has to touch it."

"But, I thought I had to bleed," Rowen said. Just standing under the sun in the middle of the Wastelands made her tired. Speaking wasn't helping. She wanted to just find a spot on the ground, curl up into a ball, and sleep.

"Just a prick of my dagger. It won't hurt for more than a few seconds."

"Not if I do it," Siddhe mumbled.

Rowen sneered at her. The mermaid had done nothing but complain during the past few days. She was literally drying out. Her skin was cracked, her hair looked brittle, and she snapped at them at every chance. She never trusted Siddhe, and feared her even more now. Rowen rubbed the place on her hand where Siddhe had once stabbed her. She knew better than anyone the consequences of Siddhe losing her temper.

Elian ignored Siddhe, and held a hand out to her, silencing her. "Please, Rowen. You're not going to be responsible for your friend's deaths. Are you?"

"If you kill them, I will never tell you," Rowen warned between clenched teeth.

Elian lowered his hands and rolled his eyes. Turning away from her, he spoke in hushed tones to Siddhe. Gavin strode over to them to join the scheming.

She was disappointed in Gavin. Why did he have to follow them?

"Don't listen to him," Feyda whispered from behind. "Run at the first chance you get."

She tensed at those words. If Feyda would risk her and her son's life to prevent Elian from finding the Red Dragon, the consequences must be dire.

She licked her lips and grimaced at the pain she felt and the blood she tasted. "Where will I run to?"

Feyda shot a glance to Elian and the others and nodded toward the mountains. "There are caves in this part. I've seen them drawn in ancient texts. Run, hide, and wait for Elian to give up. Or, snatch the map and go after the Red Dragon yourself. Just don't let him get to it. That amount of power can ruin the world."

She searched Feyda's face. The woman was serious. "How do you know all of this?"

Feyda made a face. "I know things. Trust me."

"I don't trust anyone," Rowen muttered under her breath.

Feyda nudged her. "You're going to have to trust me. Do you really think our meeting was a coincidence?"

That got her attention. "What?"

"My mission was never for the Red Dragon, dear. It was for you," she said, poking Rowen in the chest.

"Mission?"

Feyda pursed her thin lips and nodded. "That's right. There is someone more powerful and more dangerous than Captain Elian looking out for you from the shadows. Then, you'll be forced to choose and trust your greatest enemy."

"Elian?"

Feyda snorted. "Aren't you listening? Elian is no one compared to him. Elian is an old man who is sick and desperate. That does not make him your enemy."

Who that could be was a mystery. Why would anyone care to look out for her? She froze. It did make sense, though. Maybe it wasn't luck that saved her all of those times. Her mind went to the black Dragon. Her eyes widened. Whoever that was, might very well be the person Feyda warned her about.

"Think of the one person who could have orchestrated this all. Your downfall, your rescue. All of it."

She thought long and hard. The only person she could think of was Macana. She gasped. Could it be? Why would she do this? Then again, it could be King Thorne. She wavered. It was hard to focus with the weakness entering her legs.

Groaning, Rowen closed her eyes against the pain in her stomach. She rubbed her belly and nearly fell over from dizziness. Blurs of color flashed before her eyes as she lost control of her body. She could feel herself falling, but could do nothing to stop it.

Feyda caught her. Perdan helped.

"Bring the girl some food! She's going to die if you don't," Perdan shouted.

Rowen tried to stand, but before she could get a grip on her senses, Siddhe growled and stormed over to her.

She cried out as Siddhe shoved Feyda away and kicked Perdan in his stomach. "Enough of this!" She grabbed Rowen by the hair, nearly ripping it from her scalp as she dragged her over to Elian.

Snatching the map from Elian's hand, Siddhe forced it into Rowen's, and sliced her across the cheek with her dagger.

She screamed.

"Siddhe," Elian shouted. "Stop!"

"No, Captain. We're wasting time being nice," Siddhe growled and rubbed the blood from Rowen's face onto the map. "See. This is how you get stuff done."

Dumbstruck, Rowen stared at Siddhe with widened eyes and her mouth open.

She did it again. She cut her and drew blood. Rowen felt the heat rise from her toes, up her body, and to her cheeks. Her breaths came out quick and labored as she tried to control what threatened to burst free.

Your power is like a river blocked by a damn, Feyda has once said.

Enough of the abuse. Enough playing the sweet, innocent girl. Enough of it all. With a blood-curdling cry, Rowen raised her hand, with the map and flames shot out of her hand like a flood of hot red and orange.

Eyes ablaze, she glared at Siddhe, and turned the flames toward her.

Siddhe gasped and dodged her power.

The flames wouldn't stop. She couldn't stop now. All she wanted was justice and absolution. She wanted Siddhe dead.

"Rowen!" Elian shouted to her.

She could barely hear him as she slowly walked to the mermaid who cowered on the ground, her hands raised in surrender.

"Enough of this! You burnt the map!"

Rowen glared at him. "You can be next."

His jaw dropped and before Rowen could take another step, or say another word, all her power raged and roared, as her head was thrown back and it escaped through her mouth.

Rowen's eyes widened as she watched her power turn from flames, to a bright golden light.

One that lit a trail in the air. A perfect trail. Like the one on the map.

CHAPTER 18

ROWEN'S HEART RACED AS SHE looked at the others, and then at the trail she'd mapped out on the air.

Elian stepped to it, awestruck. "What?" He raked through his hair with his hands and stood there with his mouth ajar. "What did you do?"

Rowen wiped her hands on her dress and stepped away. While in the midst of using her power, she'd never felt so powerful. So unafraid. So invincible.

"I don't know," she said in a soft voice. Now, she felt exposed.

Elian looked back at her, and grinned. For a moment, he looked to her like a boy who'd just been given a new toy.

"This," he said, pointing to the trail. "Might actually work." It glittered and glowed before them, leading down the valley and to a mountain.

She thought of Feyda's words. Letting Elian get to the Red Dragon was dangerous. It could destroy the world.

A newfound energy soared inside her veins, and before Elian could do anything, Rowen ran for it. To the trail. For the Red Dragon.

She pumped her arms and worked her legs as fast as she'd ever run in her life. Not even Blackthorn and his men chasing her could make her run as fast as she did just then.

Elian ran after her, and to her surprise, he was also fast.

She took a chance and glanced over her shoulders to see Elian right on her heels. The look on his face was one of a crazed man, bent on outrunning or killing her. She screamed as he raised a hand to her.

No. She'd seen him do that before. She couldn't let him release one of his dark shadowy souls on her. So, she skidded to a stop and raised her hands back at him.

Elian, out of breath, stopped as well. "What are you going to do, Rowen?"

Rowen shook her head. She wasn't sure. But, she wasn't going to let him kill her in the middle of the Wastelands. Not after everything she'd been through. Not when she was that close to finding the Red Dragon from her prophecy.

"Just stay back," she yelled at him. Sweat beaded on her forehead and dripped into her eyes. She was ready to fight with all she had left within her.

Elia cracked a grin and raised both hands. "You don't know what you're doing, Rowen. Put your hands down, or I will have to hurt you."

"No!"

"Very well," he said, and sucked in a long breath—longer than was humanly possible. His chest seemed to expand as he did so and she feared the worst.

Come on, Rowen. Do something.

She closed her eyes and breathed in herself. She summoned her power.

Elian's cry made her open her eyes. She stumbled back and gasped as a large black Dragon with silver talons scooped Elian off the ground and threw him yards across the desert. Eyes wide, she and the others watched as the black dragon blew a ring of fire around them all.

"It's him," she said to herself as she watched him fly in her direction.

She stood her ground. Was this her savior? Her arms opened, ready to be taken away, ready to learn of his true identity.

Hope filled her belly, and a smile came to her face. Tears stung her eyes. Thank the fates for sending him.

As he flew closer, she was certain he was coming to fly her away.

Her face drained of color and a scream came from her lips as a giant red dragon flew from the clouds and tackled the black dragon in the air. She covered her mouth as the red Dragon threw the black one into the sky, and blew an intense stream of fire at him.

Feyda and Perdan ran to her, and the red Dragon noticed. He swept his wings in their way and knocked them to the ground. Then, he blew a ring of fire just around Rowen, blocking her from any chance of escape. She fell to her knees as the heat nearly blinded her vision of the fire that ensued as the black Dragon returned for another shot at the red one.

They dove and thrashed at each other, drawing blood and causing loud screeches from one another. Her poor black Dragon had his wing nipped and nearly torn in half. He spun and blew fire at it, but the red Dragon was bigger, more powerful, and closed it wings making a fire-proof shield.

Rowen looked to Elian, who lay on the ground, knocked out. Siddhe and Gavin had run to check on him. They pulled him away by his arms, and did nothing to save Rowen.

She rubbed her hands together.

Time to save myself.

She focused on clearing her head. She breathed in deep and exhaled and all sounds of the battle and the crackling fire around her faded into silence. When she opened her eyes, she tilted her head and searched for the bright energy that controlled the flames. She pulled it toward her, and then sent flames of her own to fight them. Like a dutiful subject, the flames bent to her will, and bowed before her.

She grinned and bit her bottom lips. It was working. They lowered into the ground, until not a single flame remained. She stood, and raised a hand over her eyes to block the sun's rays. She peered at the Dragons and saw that they were still in an intense battle.

If that red Dragon was the Red Dragon, she was in deep trouble.

CHAPTER 19

ROWEN'S HEART SOARED AS THE black Dragon threw its body, and all its weight into the red Dragon and knocked it from the sky. She cheered as he took the chance to fly to her. She ran to him, her hands outstretched and ready to be swept away. They were so close, and hope once again returned to tempt her.

He reached a talon toward her and she increased her speed, when something knocked her to the ground, and dug its sharp talon into her shoulder.

Rowen screamed and looked back to see the red Dragon lift her from the ground, and fly at such a speed that she could barely keep her eyes open.

"Let me go!"

The red Dragon ignored her.

She looked back as gusts of wind blew at her face. From what she could see, the black Dragon didn't have a chance at catching up and soon became nothing but a speck in the distance. It flew faster, so fast that she lost all track of where they were.

"What are you doing? Let me go," Rowen ordered. She wasn't even sure if the Dragon heard her over the raging wind. She could barely hear herself.

To make matters worse, the Dragon flew higher, so high that the air grew thin, and she started to shiver violently at the cold. She couldn't keep her eyes open as fatigue and weakness took over.

"Please," she pleaded one last time. She couldn't breathe. The air was scarce and it caused her to panic. The sound of her own heartbeat vibrated in her ears. "Please!"

The Dragon slowed, and she looked down to see a small stone city built in the top of the mountain. She realized that this was where her fire line ended. It glowed below, signaling that this was it.

The lair of the Red Dragon.

Her eyes started to flutter closed, but she fought it.

The Dragon circled around in the sky, and she wondered what he had planned. It was difficult to stay awake, but she used the last of her energy to do so. She had to see what was going to happen. What was coming.

She screamed as the Dragon opened its claws...and released her.

Her scream filled her ears and the entire mountain and valleys as she fell. The wind gripped her and pushed her down and she accelerated. To her horror, sharp rocks awaited below.

This was it. Why did her prophecies never tell her she'd die like this?

She fought the air, tried to control her screams, but the sheer terror took over and left her devoid of all thoughts. She couldn't manipulate the air like she did fire, at least not with how terrible she was at focusing at that moment. She could do nothing, but prepare herself for the pain.

She closed her eyes and wept. She hoped it would at least be quick.

All thought disappeared, and all Rowen could feel were her instincts and fire filling her veins. Then, there was the pain. She sucked in a breath as her bones started to crack and her body started to bend. She couldn't even scream through the pain. Was she dying? Had she hit the rocks? She couldn't tell. All she knew was agony.

Then, she twisted and flipped in the sky...and opened her eyes as she just skimmed the ground.

And spread her wings, catching herself.

Rowen's eyes popped open, and widened.

She blinked. "What is this?"

There was a new range of sight she'd never experienced.

"Dear fates," she squealed as she realized that her eyes were huge. She could see for miles, with such clarity that it was overwhelming.

Her heart raced.

I'm in Dragon form!

A rush of shock and excitement filled her as she flew through the sky. Her wings were massive, and beautiful. She craned her neck to get a better look at herself. She swirled in the air, and pearlescent silver aura surrounded her. She was white, with lacy swirls of scarlet decorating her wings.

She was beautiful.

She could feel herself smiling. Tears filled her eyes and she shook her head. Finally. Her one dream had come true.

She was a true Dragon.

Still, she was exhausted from running, fighting, and flying. So, she flew down to the top of the mountain and landed. Her heart nearly stopped when she realized that the Red Dragon himself had landed and stood right in front of her on his hind legs, watching her with a regal air to him that was rivalled by no king she'd ever met.

She swallowed. Just as she discovers she can shift into a Dragon, she was going to die.

She wasn't going to go down easily. She would fight.

Except...the Red Dragon didn't come after her in a rage. Instead, he tilted his giant, beautiful glowing head to the side, blinked, and studied her. Rowen wasn't sure what to say, or if he'd understand.

Then, after an excruciating moment, he gently raised his foreclaw to her face and she froze as he touched it.

He opened his mouth, and in dragontongue, said one word...

"Beloved?"

Thanks for reading! If you enjoyed this book, please consider leaving a review. Queen of the Dragons: Book Three of the Dragon-Born series is available here.

My epic fantasy, Rise of the Flame is available on Amazon here.

Six races. Four realms. One devastating war.

The survival of the universe rests on the shoulders of one human girl, but can Lilae escape slavery in time to save humanity?

An Exclusive Excerpt From *Queen of the Dragons*

THE GODS WERE NOT ON his side on this day. White cords of lightning stretched across the darkening sky as Rickard fought the gusty winds of the Wastelands in a feeble attempt to catch up to the Red Dragon. A roar emerged from his gut and out of his mouth, sending flames into the air. Full of anguish and pain, it seemed to rumble the ground below. Still, it was to no avail.

The Red Dragon had Rowen, and he was too fast, too strong, and more powerful than any Dragon Rickard had ever fought.

As Rickard watched her be swept away by the Red Dragon, his mind raced. Defeated, Rickard hovered in the air and tried to follow them with his eyes as they vanished into the gray storm clouds.

No.

Rowen slipped from his fingers. Nothing about this day was good. Not one bit.

The pain that burned in his chest was nearly debilitating. There was no way he could chase after them—not with the injury he'd suffered at the Dragon's sharp red talon. So, helpless, and with frustration overwhelming every emotion, he was forced to let her be taken.

The prophecy never said it would happen like this. There were too many factors he didn't account for. Perhaps all would be well—maybe this was as it should be.

He could only hope. He wasn't one to leave his fate in the hands of anyone but his own.

Then, he remembered something—perhaps the only thing that could help him save her.

The map.

He flew to the dusty burnt-orange dirt that spread across the entire valley of the Wastelands. With wings outstretched, he shifted back into his human form and despite the gash at his side, landed with grace.

He spat blood onto the ground and wiped his mouth with the back of his sleeve. The once stunning mermaid looked more like a beggar woman as her dark skin had dried out to a texture similar to parchment. She and the young human man stood near his dear old foe. A foe who never even knew they were in a race for the same treasure.

"Captain Elian Westin," Rickard said, crossing the distance between the two. Blond hair and bright gray eyes. He was Rowen's father all right. They even shared the same complexion, which was fairer than any Dragon in Withrae.

He would have never believed that the two were bound by blood if Nimah hadn't told him. He still grappled with that fact and had yet to make sense of it. The pirate was connected to this prophecy somehow. He just couldn't figure out how exactly.

Not yet.

The mermaid lifted her sword to him, rushing forward with a feral growl and fire in her fierce green eyes. He shot her a glare, and pushed her aside with one arm. She stumbled backward and landed on her bottom. The young man glanced down at her, held his hands up in surrender, and stepped away.

Smart lad.

Rickard stood a few inches taller than Elian, and with one hand, and the strength of his Dragon blood and that of his ancestors, he lifted the older man by his collar and narrowed his eyes. What he saw within those gray eyes that mimicked the sky before a storm was shocking, almost enough to make him lower the pirate back to the ground and leave him be.

There was such pain and torment in his eyes. Not just physical. Something deeper was buried in the human man's heart. Not only did he look older since the last time he'd seen him, but Elian was weaker.

Visibly so.

There was desperation in his eyes, and Rickard had not expected to see such a thing from the famed pirate. Everyone had heard the tales of Elian being a soul stealer. Perhaps that explained it. The man simply needed more souls.

Something told him otherwise.

Rickard searched Elian's pockets. "The map. Where is it? Hand it over."

"And, who are you supposed to be?" Elian asked, lifting a thin blond eyebrow.

Oh, you'll find out soon enough.

"Who I am is of no concern to you. Give me the map, or I break your neck."

"Without any knowledge of who you are, how can I just pass along something so powerful?"

Annoyed, and losing his patience, Rickard exhaled to calm the rage that bubbled within his gut. "I need to save the girl, you old fool."

The cackling laugh that erupted from Elian's throat did more than annoy the prince. He tightened his grip and brought Elian's face closer.

"The girl? What's she to you?" Elian asked with a laugh. "She's mine. My blood and my prize for saving her from death. Besides. The map is gone. Burned."

Burned? Chances of the day getting any better were slim.

"She may be your daughter," Rickard said, tossing Elian a few feet away. "But, she does not belong to you."

Elian crashed into the dirt and came to his knees, ready to fight.

Rickard shook his head. Sorcerer or not, the mighty pirate Captain Westin was no match for a Dragon of his strength and lineage. He looked over his shoulder to the older woman and her son as they cowered away from the two of them.

"Feyda, come," he said.

She'd removed the ropes that had bound her hands together and came to her feet. Her son, Perdan did the same. Eyeing Elian as they approached, they dusted themselves off.

"Thank the gods. You've come for us, Prince Rickard," Feyda said, bowing before him.

"What took you so long?" Perdan asked, stretching his back.

Rickard couldn't resist stealing a glance at Elian's awestruck face. A small grin came to his lips as he turned his attention back to the woman before him. She looked as though she'd suffered at Elian's hand and the terrain of the Wastelands. He hadn't a chance to get a good look at Rowen, but he hoped she hadn't been harmed.

"Tell me everything you've learned about the girl and her magic."

AVAILABLE ON AMAZON

An Exclusive Look at Spell Slinger

Proper lady by day.

Evil fighting vigilante by night.

New York Times & USA Today bestselling author, K.N. Lee presents Spell Slinger, a sci-fi fantasy romance fans are comparing to anime meets epic-fantasy.

Yara Ortuso always knew she'd follow in her father's footsteps as a Spell Slinger--until her mother sold her off as a concubine to a lord, after a forbidden romance.

Yara would have served her time as a wife to keep her family safe, but when King Loric sets a decree to abolish magic, she has no choice but to make plans for her escape.

Her best friend--a crow shifter named Hero is just what she needs. Yara vows to end the reign of murder and tyranny. But when the skeleton key transports Yara to a distant future, she must adapt to this new world. A mysterious prince with his own secret motives might stand between Yara and her quest for vengeance.

The future is an alluring and mysterious place, where the effects of a world without magic is apparent by the rise in supernatural activity--and King Loric still lives.

Chapter 1

FEAR THREATENED TO CRIPPLE YARA as she passed the servants harvesting the grapes of Torrington Orchard.

It was a cool autumn morning, and yet Yara felt sweat bead on her forehead and in the crease between her bosom.

"Good morning, my lady," one of the workers said, bowing her bonnet-covered head.

She feigned a smile, and yet her heart pounded inside her chest as she hid the blood that stained her bodice by letting her long white hair hang over her narrow shoulders.

Be brave, Yara thought as she wrung her shaking hands.

"Hero," she spoke to the wind. "Please get me out of here. I'm serious this time."

Yara broke into a run toward the stables, no longer caring who she vexed by her sudden action. She didn't have much time. The body would surely be found at any moment.

The sun warmed her cold cheeks as she looked to the sky.

Come on, Hero. Hurry.

She grabbed her long navy skirts into her fists as her feet pounded the stone path that led to the front gate. Soldiers stood guard on either end of the locked gate, their swords secure at the waist.

A squawking sound came from the distance and Yara snatched off the silver band on her finger—the one that marked her as property of the sheriff—and tossed it into the bushes that lined the road.

Her heart thumped in her chest as one of the soldiers glanced her way. He narrowed his eyes at her. "Where are you going?"

She ignored him, keeping her attention fixed on that gate. They'd hang her if she ever got caught, but she had to risk it.

A royal decree was announced.

Magic is abolished.

All Spell Slingers are to be executed.

Those with magic must go to the capital of Allarya for evaluation.

Those who resist will be executed.

There was no way she could stand by and let her father be executed. Life as a concubine was over for Yara. It was time to stop running from her destiny.

To be a Spell Slinger.

A grin came to her face, despite the tears that trailed down her cheeks as a tall young man dressed in all black appeared outside of the gate, his pale skin almost translucent as he held a hand out toward her.

Black hair covered his eyes. Clean shaven, and baby-faced, Hero was her greatest friend, one that would risk his life to save hers.

She chewed her lip, quickening her pace as she prayed that they would both survive this.

"Ay," the guard shouted, drawing his sword. "Stop right now, miss. We don't want to have to hurt you."

Yara ignored them. She had been hurt enough. The bruises on her neck were proof enough.

At that moment, she needed every bit of concentration to do what she'd been planning for the past few days. She would have served her time in this horrid place for all eternity if they'd have left her family alone.

The king wanted to abolish magic, and no one could stop him.

Except Yara.

She gritted her teeth and with a burst of energy shot outside of her body, a blue aura encircling her as her soul unfused.

Hero cracked a grin, his eyes narrowing behind strands of black hair. "Good girl," he whispered, a black mist shooting from his hand and reaching for her like a raging wind.

The soldiers stumbled backward, having never seen such a display of raw power.

As if encased in ice, Yara's entire body went cold as her soul left it behind. Her body was indeed frozen in place as her consciousness rode her soul out of the magic-bonded gate.

No human, shifter, or sorcerer could exit that gate.

But, a Meta could.

Born half sorceress, and half Meta, Yara could do many things that the world had never even heard of.

As Hero pulled her soul to his open palm, she felt safe and warm, having shed her human form.

Once through the gate, he tucked her soul into his body and shifted into a crow.

Soon, Torrington Estate would be far behind them, and Yara would need to create herself a new body.

Chapter 2

YARA NEVER EXPECTED TO BE sold off to the county sheriff as his tenth concubine. At twenty-one, she was broken mentally and emotionally, and now without a father.

Too late.

This was her entire reason for exposing herself and running away from Torrington Manor. Having heard that King Loric was targeting Spell Slingers, she'd had no choice but to at least try to save her father.

Tears welled in her eyes as she looked at her father's body, hanging from the fir tree in front of her family's mountain cabin.

At least they didn't burn him.

She glanced at Hero as he waited up in a tree. His crow form was a blessing when outlawed in seven counties.

Yara was thankful for such a loyal friend. He'd rescued her and kept her safe while she summoned the energy to recreate her old body. While she fought the fever that came with a new body, he cared for her in his cabin.

"If you'd have come back just yesterday, you might have caught him before the execution," a familiar voice called from beside her a few feet away.

Yara wiped her face dry with her sleeve and turned to see Pae standing there, her arms folded across her green dress.

"I told you our time's running up. I suspect magic will be no more within a few years," she said, her white hair lifting with the crisp fall breeze.

Though she was fifteen years older than Yara, they could have been twins.

Silver eyes that matched Yara's looked her up and down.

Though Yara was fully dressed in leather pants tucked into her boots, and a black shirt with a hood that covered her bright hair, she felt naked under her gaze.

Always had.

"If you hadn't of sold me, I could have protected you both."

"I did what I had to—to protect the family from you." Pae looked cross, her eyes narrowed, her hair lifting with a passing breeze. "Where is your husband?"

"Dead," Yara quipped. "And a concubine is not considered a wife, Pae. So, he wasn't my husband."

Pae tilted her head. Her face paled. "Did you kill him?"

"I did what I had to."

"Dear spirits."

"He deserved it."

"What is wrong with you, Yara? You can't kill a man for beating you now and again. Especially if he owns you."

"Of course, you think so," Yara said. "You beat me plenty whilst I was growing up. And why? Father never raised a hand to you."

"That's different," Pae said. "I'm your mum. And pain is the only way children learn."

Frowning, she turned back to her father. Someone had stolen his shoes.

"Why is he still hanging? I'm grabbing an ax and cutting him down."

"You do that, and they will use that ax to chop off your head." Pae sighed, her body becoming more and more translucent with each minute.

Yara stared at her wondering if she ever loved her father. Growing up, they never showed affection for each other. It was as if they were no more than business partners, come together to raise one shy girl with too much power to be allowed around others.

"You'd best be on your way out of Kempsey. They're determined to abolish magic. That means Spell Slingers everywhere are being strung up."

"I'll leave after I bury him."

Pae sighed. "Stubborn girl. Give me a minute, and I'll help."

"Don't you need to get out of the sun?"

"I'm fine. I can last a while longer," Pae said, her voice growing distant as if she'd be carried away by the wind.

Being a Meta, Pae was a creature of the night. Sometimes Yara thought she'd just used her father for his power, to remain a solid being in the human world—instead of a woman that resembled a ghost more than an actual person.

They buried Bronson behind the cabin, and Pae even sang a little song from her world for him.

"Bye, Pae," Yara said, slinging her pack over her shoulders and heading for the paved road that led to the main highway.

"Yara, wait! Where do you think you're going?"

"The capital."

"Allarya? Why?"

Yara glanced back at her, fire in her silver eyes. "To kill King Loric. Either come along or leave me be."

Pae's eyes widened. "Have you gone mad?"

"No," Yara said, turning to look ahead.

Allarya was far from their little rural village, but she owed her father revenge. She owed their entire kingdom a chance at a better life.

"I'm not mad, Mother. I've just gained some courage," she whispered.

Chapter 3

THE DUSTY ROAD AHEAD WAS a constant reminder of the life Yara was leaving behind. It was also a beacon of hope.

Yara twisted her long white hair into a bun at the top of her head and yawned. She hadn't slept in what felt like days. Using so much energy to recreate her body had taken more out of her than she would have liked. She just hoped that there would be no trouble on the road. This new body was weak, and would need a few days to be able to defend itself.

Knowing that Hero was close by gave her a small measure of relief. Sharing a body was such an intimate experience, and she would forever be bound to Hero because of it. They could summon one another whenever they pleased, and that fact was a source of comfort she'd cherish forever.

Dark clouds started to roll by. A storm was brewing, and she knew that it brewed for her.

Watching. Searching. Ready to strike her dead.

If she could stop King Loric along with his laws and reign of terror, she would be free to live her own life for once. As long as she didn't get herself killed.

Death frightened her more than anything.

Tears streamed down her face as she remembered her father's last hug. It had been longer than usual, and full of love that she knew he had for her. Neither could have known that it would be the last one that they would share.

Pae had never hugged Yara in that way, and it was because of her that she'd been sent to a form of slavery most young women in Allarya knew all too well.

One day, they'd have a choice of who they married and wouldn't become concubines or slaves. Another reason King Lori needed to be stopped.

The screeching of a crow stopped Yara in her tracks.

Hero.

She wiped her tears with the back of her hand and sniffled.

"Are you all right, Yara?" He asked her as he landed on the road, and returned to his human form.

"No," she said. "I'm really not. I miss him, Hero."

His brows furrowed as he walked beside her. "I know. He was the kindest man I've ever met. Except Red."

Yara tensed at the mention of Red, the gamekeeper of Westerbrook Manor.

"It's fine," she said, sniffling. "I will avenge him."

Hero fell into stride with her. He wrapped an arm around her shoulders and she wished she could melt into his warmth once again. "We will avenge him. Together. You know I'd do anything for you, don't you?"

She glanced at him. He raked his slick black hair out of his face, revealing green eyes that matched the meadows behind her house in the hills. His face was narrow and pointed at the chin, but nice to look at.

"Of course, I do. I'd do that same for you."

His smile warmed her heart. Why couldn't she smile like that? Happiness was a foreign emotion for Yara.

"So," Hero began, looking ahead at the long, winding road. "What is the plan?"

"We make our way to the castle, and I show Loric what the last Spell Slinger is capable of."

Hero nodded. "I'm eager to witness this. But, I fear this world isn't ready for what you're capable of. Perhaps we should think of another strategy."

"No. This is personal. I want to kill him myself."

"Slow down there. I know exactly how you feel, but you're not a killer."

"I killed the sheriff."

Hero stopped walking. He took Yara by the arms and turned her to him. "Yes. You protected yourself. If you hadn't used your power, he would have stolen your precious life."

Yara looked away, tears welling in her eyes. She'd never been so afraid in her life. Even growing up with a meta for a mother, with fear of the dark in her heart, she'd never experienced what it felt like to almost die. The sheriff had wrapped his hands around her neck the instant she'd proclaimed that she was leaving, and didn't let go.

Until Yara sucked the life from his body with her power.

She sighed. "I am tired of feeling like this, Hero."

He took her face into his hands and gazed into her eyes. "You know, we can escape to another kingdom. We can put all of this behind us."

Yara stepped away from him. "No. King Loric has to be stopped. Running isn't an option."

She turned and started back down the road, wiping her tears, and putting on a brave face.

As she approached the sign that marked the edge of town, she paused.

"What's wrong?"

Yara glanced back at Hero. "Nothing. I was just thinking of Asher. I never got a chance to say goodbye."

"Look, Yara. I wasn't going to tell you, but I thought you should know. It might even cheer you up...if even for a little bit."

Yara squinted at him. "Tell me."

"Asher's joining the royal army. He leaves tomorrow. I thought you'd want to say goodbye to one more person. Seeing as we might not ever come back and all..." he said, his voice trailing.

"Dear spirits," Yara said, looking down the road. She scratched her chin, torn.

Westerbrook Manor wasn't far. She might be able to stop by and see Asher. Truth was, she wasn't sure if she was strong enough to say goodbye to him—despite their memories together being the only thing that helped her make it through the day.

"Thank you," she said and chewed her lip.

She had to see him. One last time.

!

AN EXCLUSIVE LOOK AT

QUEEN Of the DRAGONS

K.N. LEE

CHAPTER ONE

The gods were not on his side on this day. White cords of lightning stretched across the darkening sky as Rickard fought the gusty winds of the Wastelands in a feeble attempt to catch up to the Red Dragon. A roar emerged from his gut and out of his mouth, sending flames into the air. Full of anguish and pain, it seemed to rumble the ground below. Still, it was to no avail.

The Red Dragon had Rowen, and he was too fast, too strong, and more powerful than any Dragon Rickard had ever fought.

As Rickard watched her be swept away by the Red Dragon, his mind raced. Defeated, Rickard hovered in the air and tried to follow them with his eyes as they vanished into the gray storm clouds.

No.

Rowen slipped from his fingers. Nothing about this day was good. Not one bit.

The pain that burned in his chest was nearly debilitating. There was no way he could chase after them—not with the injury he'd suffered at the Dragon's sharp red talon. So, helpless, and with frustration overwhelming every emotion, he was forced to let her be taken.

The prophecy never said it would happen like this. There were too many factors he didn't account for. Perhaps all would be well—maybe this was as it should be.

He could only hope. He wasn't one to leave his fate in the hands of anyone but his own.

Then, he remembered something—perhaps the only thing that could help him save her.

The map.

He flew to the dusty burnt-orange dirt that spread across the entire valley of the Wastelands. With arms wings outstretched, he shifted back into his human form and despite the gash at his side, landed with grace.

He spat blood onto the ground and wiped his mouth with the back of his sleeve. The once stunning mermaid looked more like a beggar woman as her dark skin had dried out to a texture similar to parchment. She and the young human man stood near his dear old foe. A foe who never even knew they were in a race for the same treasure.

"Captain Elian Westin," Rickard said, crossing the distance between the two. Blond hair and bright gray eyes. He was Rowen's father all right. They even shared the same complexion, which was fairer than any Dragon in Withrae.

He would have never believed that the two were bound by blood if Nimah hadn't told him. He still grappled with that fact and had yet to make sense of it. The pirate was connected to this prophecy somehow. He just couldn't figure out how exactly.

Not yet.

The mermaid lifted her sword to him, rushing forward with a feral growl and fire in her fierce amber eyes. He shot her a glare, and pushed her aside with one arm. She stumbled backward and landed on her bottom. The young man glanced down at her, held his hands up in surrender, and stepped away.

Smart lad.

Rickard stood a few inches taller than Elian, and with one hand, and the strength of his Dragon blood and that of his ancestors, he lifted the older man by his collar and narrowed his eyes. What he saw within those gray eyes that mimicked the sky before a storm was shocking, almost enough to make him lower the pirate back to the ground and leave him be.

There was such pain and torment in his eyes. Not just physical. Something deeper was buried in the human man's heart. Not only did he look older since the last time he'd seen him, but Elian was weaker.

Visibly so.

There was desperation in his eyes, and Rickard had not expected to see such a thing from the famed pirate. Everyone had heard the tales of Elian being a soul stealer. Perhaps that explained it. The man simply needed more souls.

Something told him otherwise.

Rickard searched Elian's pockets. "The map. Where is it? Hand it over."

"And, who are you supposed to be?" Elian asked, lifting a thin blond eyebrow.

Oh, you'll find out soon enough.

"Who I am is of no concern to you. Give me the map, or I break your neck."

"Without any knowledge of who you are, how can I just pass along something so powerful?"

Annoyed, and losing his patience, Rickard exhaled to calm the rage that bubbled within his gut. "I need to save the girl, you old fool."

The cackling laugh that erupted from Elian's throat did more than annoy the prince. He tightened his grip and brought Elian's face closer.

"The girl? What's she to you?" Elian asked with a laugh. "She's mine. My blood and my prize for saving her from death. Besides. The map is gone. Burned."

Burned? Chances of the day getting any better were slim.

"She may be your daughter," Rickard said, tossing Elian a few feet away. "But, she does not belong to you."

Elian crashed into the dirt and came to his knees, ready to fight.

Rickard shook his head. Sorcerer or not, the mighty pirate Captain Westin was no match for a Dragon of his strength and lineage. He looked over his shoulder to the older woman and her son as they cowered away from the two of them.

"Feyda, come," he said.

She'd removed the ropes that had bound her hands together and came to her feet. Her son, Perdan did the same. Eyeing Elian as they approached, they dusted themselves off.

"Thank the gods. You've come for us, Prince Rickard," Feyda said, bowing before him.

"What took you so long?" Perdan asked, stretching his back.

Rickard couldn't resist stealing a glance at Elian's awestruck face. A small grin came to his lips as he turned his attention back to the woman before him. She looked as though she'd suffered at Elian's hand and the terrain of the Wastelands. He hadn't a chance to get a good look at Rowen, but he hoped she hadn't been harmed.

"Tell me everything you've learned about the girl and her magic."

CHAPTER TWO

I am a Dragon. A real Dragon.

Those words resounded in Rowen's head as she flew through the clouds. The landscape below was stunning. Dark orange terrain with rocky golden and silver mountains jutting high into the sky.

Gusts of wind blew at Rowen and propelled her faster through the sky. Exhilaration filled her veins, and she closed her eyes for a moment to enjoy the fresh scent of the cool air, and its feel on her face and under her wings.

Still, she was left with uncertainty. When she opened her eyes, she caught a glimpse of the Red Dragon. He chased her, and as she watched him keep pace with her, she wondered if he was friend or foe. At least she was also a Dragon and stood a better chance at defending herself in this form.

But, why was she here? Her memory struggled to put faded pieces together. The animalistic part of her brain threatened to take over, and erase all memories. She couldn't let that happen.

She had to be stronger—to fight the force that tried to control her.

The Red Dragon gained speed and flew beside her, and a vivid image of it picking her up from the ground returned.

Then, there was the word beloved that came from his lips. What did he mean by that?

Rowen now remembered. That one word made her lose control and shift into a dragon again.

Now, how to change back?

First, she needed to find somewhere to land. Or, she could run. But, who would teach her about this new form? Mother! Broken images of her mother came back to her. Yes, she was beautiful. She remembered that much. And, she loved Rowen. She was one of the only people Rowen knew she could trust.

If only she knew how to get home to Harrow. But wait— the Duke would surely turn her in. She shuddered as a full memory began to form.

Dragons hunted her. She'd escaped death.

Twice.

The Red Dragon spoke to her. Mind to mind. His voice was jarring, and suppressed all of her thoughts. It seeped into every crevice of her mind. So much so that she feared he could read all of her thoughts, not just when she needed to speak directly to him.

"Enough of this. We need to talk."

"Who are you?"

"You don't remember? Do you?" The Red Dragon asked. "Come, land over here. You'll be able to think much better in your human form. The Dragon magic is too strong for you right now. You need to practice."

"Just let me fly," Rowen said, going higher. "I've wanted to fly my entire life. I can't believe this is real."

"What do you mean? You've never flown before?"

She turned to him and gave a nod. If only he knew how emotional the sensation of being free to fly in the air was for her. She'd spent countless hours trying to to shift into her Dragon form, to no avail. After years of trying, she'd given up and forgotten her dream to be a true Dragon.

Her dream had come true. She could manipulate fire. She could fly. Now, she wondered what else she could do.

"We can fly later," he said.

Before she could protest, he corralled her forward, and then down toward the mountain top. He was stronger, bigger, and determined to bend her to his will.

Defenseless, he pushed her down with the force and weight of his massive foot. Before she could control what was happening, she shifted back into her human form. Now, the difference in size was unfathomable. The Red Dragon towered above her, as tall as the trees that stood outside her manor back in Harrow.

Exposed, and fragile, she looked up into his large eyes and swallowed back her fear.

"Don't eat me," she squealed as he licked the blood from her cheek where Siddhe had stabbed her.

He snorted, a puff of smoke coming from his nostrils. "Eat you?" As he leaned down to sniff her, she closed her eyes.

Shifting Dragons weren't known for eating humans, but if the Red Dragon was the ancient kind, that was another story. Legends told of the occasional human meal.

Her body tensed at the cold touch of his nose on her face. She never imagined she'd get eaten by a Dragon. By the size of him, she'd be little more than a snack.

She gasped as he withdrew and lifted her with a single talon before his face.

He peered at her, and she held her breath.

This was it. Her heart thumped in her chest. She'd faced death far too many times, yet it didn't get easier.

The silence that passed between them was unbearable. Then, he dropped her back to the dirt and stones.

"Not beloved," he whispered. "Who then?"

Rowen looked up at him, relieved. Maybe she wouldn't be eaten today. "That's right," she said. "I'm sorry, but I'm not this beloved you speak of."

"Who then?" The Red Dragon asked, raising his voice. The pebbles and stones on the ground rose and the ground shook.

Rowen opened her mouth to answer him. It snapped shut, and she frowned. Her mind had grown blank. Her throat tightened with dread.

"I can't remember."

CHAPTER THREE

Prince Rickard?

"I knew there was something odd going on here," Siddhe whispered.

Elian held up a hand to silence her as his mind put all of the pieces together.

They know each other.

Elian's jaw tightened as he watched Feyda approach Rickard and address him as Prince. He should have known that the sorceress before him hadn't encountered Rowen coincidentally. In his experience, coincidences didn't exist. With the new crown prince of Withrae in the way, he had to rethink his strategy.

"How much were you able to teach Rowen before Elian and his cronies arrived?" Rickard asked.

"So, you've been meddling this entire time, haven't you?" Elian asked. He glared at the young Dragon. "Your highness."

Rickard grinned. "I told you. You know nothing."

"I know that my map and my daughter have nothing to do with you."

"That'll be enough put of you. Elian," Feyda said. "Sit down."

Elian titled his head and narrowed his eyes at her. "Make me, old woman."

She put her hands on her hips. "Now, no one wants to see me get violent. Least of all, you. We've been here before. Don't forget it."

"I should have killed you when I had the chance," Elian said, seething with anger. Her soul would do very nicely with his collection.

"Perhaps," Feyda said, clasping her hands before her. "But, you didn't. Your mistake."

Siddhe tugged at his sleeve. Her voice came in a soft whisper. "We need to get out of here."

Elian knew she was right. But, his desire to hear the answer to Rickard's question was stronger than his desire to escape.

"She's a fast learner," Feyda told Rickard. "She learned how to manipulate fire faster than a second year sorcery novice. In just days, Rickard. Days."

Rubbing his chin, a brief sense of relief seemed to wash over Rickard's face. That intrigued Elian. Why was he involved at all?

"Good," Rickard said. "So, she may be able to defend herself if the need presents itself?"

Feyda pursed her lips and her brows rose. "She can do more than that. I guarantee you, that girl is more powerful than all of us combined. She just needs to trust in the magic that flows within."

"Interesting," Rickard said. "How powerful, exactly?"

A ghost of a smile came to Feyda's lips as Elian watched her look to the sky.

"The girl can summon Dragon's fire in her human form. That's how powerful she is. And, I sense much more there that has not yet been revealed."

That made Elian stand up straight. Eyes widened, he followed Feyda's gaze to the sky. How did he make such a powerful young woman? Did she truly inherit both his sorcery and the power of her mother's Dragon line?

"But, she cannot shift? Correct?" Rickard asked.

Feyda nodded. "As far as I know, if a Dragon hasn't shifted by puberty, it won't happen at all."

Rickard turned to Elian. "Now, old man. What do you want with the Red Dragon? What makes you so desparate to chase such a prophecy?"

"Prophecy?" Elian asked, shaking his head. He wondered just how much the prince knew.

"Don't pretend as though you don't know about the power of the Red Dragon. Why else would you search for it your entire life?" Rickard asked. "Nimah's told me all about you."

Elian's eye twitched.

Nimah.

Why was she involved?

Perdan stepped forward. "That's easy," he said, drawing everyone's attention. "I can answer that one, your highness. Elian wants to swallow the Red Dragon's power and become the most powerful wizard to ever live."

Elian glared at Perdan. "What do you know, besides the taste of a man's lips? Adults are talking here, little boy."

Perdan's cheeks grew bright red, but he kept his mouth pursed and stood closer to his mother.

"Why else would you want the Red Dragon's power?" Feyda asked, putting her arm around her son's shoulders. "I think Perdan is on the right path here."

Shrugging, Elian remained silent. Why reveal to them that it was not power he desired?

It was time—and as the pain in his chest started to spread, it was clear that he was running out of it.

"Well, that simply will not do," Rickard said, clearly agitated for some reason. "Tie them up, and head back to Kabrick. Wait for me there."

"As you wish, Prince Rickard," Feyda said, as Perdan walked over to do as they were told. "What are you going to do?"

Elian watched Rickard look to the sky and followed his gaze.

"I'm going to go and find Rowen."

An Exclusive Look at
Rise
of the
Flame

Prologue

EVEN IN THE LOWEST LEVELS of the Aurorian palace, where the servants slept, the castle staff sat up and listened to the queen's cries of pain. No one wanted her to die. She was only the fourth queen of the Black Throne, and yet she was the most loved.

King Torek paced the dim, narrow corridor; the only light came from the brass torches placed against the stone walls. His brow furrowed as he waited for his summons.

He wondered if it had been wise of them to try for a second child. He was growing older and weaker. But one son wasn't enough of a legacy for an Aurorian king. Torek had grown up with four brothers and seven sisters.

The time for doubts had passed. They were twenty hours into labor, and either the child would finally come or both the baby and the mother would die.

King Torek sat down on the carpeted corridor's floor in exhaustion. His legs were tired from standing. Sweat ran down his balding scalp.

"Do you need anything, sire?"

King Torek waved the young guard away as one last scream, more agonizing than the rest, broke him from his thoughts. Torek drew a fearful breath and waited.

After a few moments of complete silence, the short midwife opened the doors to Queen Sysil's quarters and ushered him inside.

The air inside the room was thick and steamy, the candlelight dim; it bathed the room in a faint orange glow. The smell of blood and sweat invaded his nostrils, so he covered his nose with his long velvet sleeve.

King Torek noticed his young wife sprawled motionless on the bed. "Is she all right?" A look of worry creased his aging face.

Queen Sysil's eyes seemed sealed shut from tears of pain. Her scarlet hair was in disarray and sweat beaded her pale face. Her chest rose slightly and fell, and he sighed in relief.

The midwife nodded. "She's only resting." Her aged eyes seemed to hold something more.

"Where's the child?" His dark eyes roamed the room. There were no screams or cries from the baby.

The midwife pointed a chubby finger to the small bassinet at the queen's bedside. The midwife's aide stepped aside timidly, careful to avoid eye contact as the king towered over them on his path to the baby.

An attendant wiped the sweat from the queen's face with a cool rag. Sysil's lips trembled. "I am sorry that it is a girl. We can try again, if it is your desire."

If only they had time to try again. Sysil was only twenty-two, but Torek was nearly seventy, and his body reminded him of his mortality every day. Two children would have to do.

"A baby girl?" To everyone's surprise, Torek smiled.

He looked in at the daughter who seemed so calm and peaceful. He picked her up, and his thoughts of having another boy vanished as he stared at her appealing yet eerie beauty.

The girl was tiny with a head full of short, curly hair. He'd never seen anyone with hair that shade of red before. It was so bright that it seemed to have traces of gold throughout.

The king's body tensed as though under a spell when his daughter looked up into his eyes. Under long, thick golden lashes she had eyes of a rich, bluish green. He gasped, almost dropping her, when a faint flicker of light moved deeply within them. The child yawned innocently, her little mouth opening in a perfect circle, before she closed her eyes to sleep.

"Do not look too deeply into the child's eyes."

"She's bewitched," one of the attendants whispered.

Torek turned and looked at the midwife; one of his bushy white eyebrows rose in search of answers. The queen's attendants avoided his eyes as they busied themselves with cleaning the room of the blood-soaked rags.

The babe did indeed resemble the queen as far as her hair color; however, her blue-green eyes were rare and unsettling. Though many humans of the North had special traits, there was something more to this girl.

Torek already felt a deep love for the child, his baby girl. He gently hugged her close to him.

"Let me hold her, your grace." The midwife held her arms out, her small eyes never leaving the baby.

"My king, what is wrong?" Sysil weakly tried to sit up in the bed. Her face paled even more when she saw Torek's smile fade.

The child's eyes... did that thing again, flickering with light. Torek swallowed hard, fearing that something was wrong. He watched as the midwife examined the baby, the room full of tension.

Heavy boots trampling down the corridor broke the silence. The door burst open, and the captain of the palace guards, Pirin, charged into the room.

"What is going on?"

Pirin pointed to the midwife. "Get the child from that woman! She is a witch." Pirin looked to the king and spoke quickly. "We found the real midwife's body in the stables." He glared at the woman who stood there with the princess in her arms.

There was a collective gasp from the aides.

"I've been called many things over the centuries, but never a witch."

Torek's heart raced as he watched the midwife transform to a woman of a younger age. He stepped back, startled. His jaw hung open as his eyes searched her face. Torek balled up his fists as rage filled his veins.

She did look evil with her black hair and pale skin. Her blue eyes looked at him without fear and that made his anger intensify. She stood there holding his beloved daughter.

"I assure you," she said, "I am Delia, Elder and gatekeeper of the Underworld. Not even a witch is safe from my power. Now, lower your weapons and listen to me."

"Sorcery! Seize her!"

Delia shook her head, gripping the baby close to her chest. "I have not come to harm the child." She raised a hand as if to calm them, meeting all of their eyes.

"Seize her!" The soldiers charged for her.

The calamity and uproar upset the wee princess, who wailed into the air.

"Silence!" With a flick of her small hand, Delia seemed to rip their voices right from their throats. It was so sudden and immobilizing that no one could even scream. The room was flooded by light, and all sound was sucked away. When she lowered her hand, everyone was frozen in place like a statue.

Delia slumped onto a chair, exhausted from her sudden burst of energy. She looked down at the child whose cry was the only sound heard in the room. She sighed and gently rubbed the girl's tiny hand, as if to soothe her.

"I warned you," Delia said, shaking her head. "I have come a long, long way to help you humans."

Torek watched as Delia gazed into his daughter's eyes. He saw the woman's body shiver and knew that she, too, saw the light flicker there.

"The Ancients have asked me to protect this child, and, as an Elder, I am more qualified than any of you to help her fulfill her destiny."

The veins in Torek's neck strained as he watched the woman cradling his daughter. Elder or not, he wanted to break free from the hold she had on all of them and wring her neck.

She reached inside her leather side-purse for a clear vial of blue liquid. When she opened the cask, a slight cloud of frost escaped. Torek watched as Delia drank a tiny sip; she squeezed her eyes shut and breathed deeply, as if waiting for something to happen. Finally, she stood.

"Listen, Torek. You should be glad that I arrived first." She wrapped the baby in a blanket and secured her to a sling upon her chest. "I don't have the time to explain everything, but you have to know that others will come, if the child stays here. You have to trust me."

Delia knew that she was asking the impossible of Torek and Sysil.

"Our world is about to change," Delia said. "There are beings who would seek to kill the princess and destroy your kingdom. Understand that I will protect her, train her, and prepare her for the time when she will be called upon to save our world."

Delia looked toward the captain of the guards; he was tall like most Aurorians and very well built. "Pirin, is it?" His eyes widened. "I shall take you with me. Lilae will need training, and—" She looked him over. "—you will do."

Delia released Pirin from his frozen state, and he fell to the floor. His hair was so blond that it was nearly white, and it fell into his eyes as he looked up at her. He winced as he began to move his limbs, as if shaking out pins and needles. He stretched his arms and picked up his sword.

"What do you mean, 'will do'?" Pirin frowned at her, furrowing his thin eyebrows. "I haven't agreed to anything."

"Do you understand that you have been chosen to join the child and me?"

Torek looked around at the others, whose eyes were now glazed over; he sensed that they were no longer aware of what was occurring.

"Why?" Pirin asked. "You're still an enemy as far as I'm concerned. I know you have power. I've seen that. But try to harm the king and queen, and I will find a way to kill you."

Delia blinked at him and sighed. "I know you have no reason to trust me, but in time the Ancients will reveal to you what I have seen."

Pirin stood there and glanced at the king.

"The Ancients created the races who populate the world, and they have put their trust in this me. Can you understand this?"

"You're obviously not from Auroria," Pirin reasoned, his eyes grazing over her dark hair. "You don't have our pure blood, nor fair hair and light eyes." Though Delia's eyes were blue, they were dark, like the ocean at night. "But you haven't come all of this way just to kill the child, either. That is what I understand."

"I have not, Pirin. But there are those who would come from afar to do just that. I wish to protect the child from those with power, who would use it to kill her. She is a weapon that, if in the wrong hands, could cause great harm to this world."

"You are really an Elder?" Pirin remained calm, looking at the woman who claimed to have once ruled the Underworld.

"I am."

Pirin frowned. "You don't look like an Elder."

"Have you ever seen an Elder?"

He shook his head.

"Good. And you don't want to see me in my true form." She watched his face. "Pirin, look at me."

He glanced up at her.

"I will tell you everything you need to know after we are far from danger."

"What danger?"

"I don't think you are quite ready to know such things," she said. "But in time, I will tell you."

Though Pirin's stance looked imposing, his eyes filled with worry. "I need more than that, Elder. I have a wife and two little girls. What will become of them? Who will protect them if I come with you and the princess?"

"Bring them," Delia said without hesitation. "We will give this child a family and protect her until her time has come."

"Do I have a choice?"

"You do. But wouldn't you still be serving your king and queen by protecting their daughter?"

Pirin looked up. "Yes, but I'd be putting my twin daughters in harm's way."

Delia lifted her shoulders. "Are there any other soldiers who could do as good of a job protecting and training the princess as you?"

He shook his head.

"And wouldn't it be wise to keep your family close, to protect and train them as you would the princess?"

Pirin looked back at his men. They were still frozen.

"I know your secret, Pirin..."

His face lost what little color it had when his eyes lifted to hers. "What?"

"You heard me."

He shifted from one foot to another. "What do you think you know?"

"I know everything." There was a tense silence between them, as she watched him with a straight face. "So, are you coming or not?"

"I'll do it."

Delia nodded, a small smile forming at the corners of her lips. "Are you doing it because I know all of your secrets, or because you want to?"

"Everyone has secrets. I care about the child. You have given me a chance to protect her, and I accept."

"Well said. I see much good in you, Pirin. You will go down in history for your part in this."

Pirin put his sword away and looked at the queen, whose tears were trailing down her face. "I don't care about history. I only care about this child and my own. If what you say is true about danger heading this way, then we'd better get going."

Pirin crossed the room and wiped the queen's face. He leaned down and whispered something to her. Pirin unhooked Sysil's silver necklace and balled it into his fist.

Delia narrowed her eyes and asked, "What exactly are you doing?"

Pirin turned, his hazel eyes wet. "For the princess. She will need a token from her mother. It's the least we can do, isn't it?"

Delia nodded, staring at the necklace for a moment before putting her hand across the baby's face. Instantaneously, the little girl fell asleep.

"One more question, Elder?"

"Call me Delia, please," she replied to Pirin.

He nodded, dropping the necklace into his pocket. "Fine... Delia." He lifted his shoulders in a shrug and asked, "Why me?"

Delia pulled on her cloak and covered the girl's head, holding her snuggly against her chest. She walked toward the door but glanced back at Pirin, an eerie smile on her pale face.

"It was always you, Pirin. Coincidences don't just happen. We have all been chosen, so long ago that the world has forgotten. We cannot escape our fate; not when the entire world is at stake."

LILAE FLOATED BARE-SKINNED beneath the bright crescent moon, her arms outstretched on the lake's calm surface. Winter never seemed to end in northern Eura, but she braved the frigid water for the solitude offered by an evening swim.

Alone, she thought, just how I like it.

Just as she began to relax, Lilae felt the presence of her Elder in the black shadows of the forest.

This is not good. She peeked over and saw Delia in the human form she'd stolen when she was forced to leave the Underworld, her pale face illuminated from beneath the hood of her wool cloak. She held her wooden staff in one hand and Lilae's discarded cloak in the other.

"Lilae!"

Lilae swallowed and then flipped over to swim back toward the shore, closing the gap between them. She quickly got out of the water and dressed, taking the heavy cloak from Delia's grasp and flinging it over her shoulders to ward off the chill in the air.

"What is it? What's happened?" Her breath escaped her lips like a puff of smoke in the darkness.

Delia looked over Lilae with dull blue eyes. "I don't like how close they are getting. We need to leave before dawn."

Lilae tucked her boyish pants into her boots. Only a few years ago, she would have refused; she would have run away to stay with another family in their village. Now, at almost eighteen, Lilae resigned herself to their nomadic lifestyle.

That's because she had finally learned why they moved so much: Lilae was being hunted.

Lilae followed Delia through the forest to their little cottage on the edge of town. It was a small structure, built into the side of a hill. Though it was once a cave, Pirin had made it into a real home. A squat chimney protruded from beneath the soil, a trail of smoke wafting from its mouth into the gray sky.

Lilae ducked as she stepped inside. Pirin, Lhana, and the twins, Risa and Jaiza, were already awake. Her surrogate family. They glanced at her and, without a word, returned to their preparations. They all moved slowly as the cold air in the room bit at them.

Pirin put his arm around Lhana. She stopped packing and buried her tears in his shoulder, sighing. "Just tell me why? Every time we finally get comfortable and make friends, you make us leave."

He smoothed her blonde hair and kissed her cheek. "And every time you ask me this same question. The answer will not change. They are coming. We don't have time to waste."

"Let us stay behind. It's not the girls and me that he wants."

Pirin grabbed Lhana by the elbow. The room fell silent, and Lilae tensed, her eyes darting from Lhana's stunned face to Pirin's stern expression.

Pirin lowered his voice, but Lilae heard every word. "We stay together. She is my responsibility."

Lhana swallowed and arched a brow, her jaw clenched. Her eyes may have glared in defiance, but her voice wavered. "I thought she was the Elder's responsibility. You trained her. Your duty is done."

Pirin pulled Lhana closer. "I will not hear another word about it." The discussion was over. Pirin's word was law. Everyone went back to packing.

Lilae glanced at Lhana and wondered if the Ancients knew how much Lhana hated her. Lhana met Lilae's eyes with what was clearly resentment. It was a look that hurt Lilae more than anything; there was almost nothing she wanted more than to finally feel that woman's love.

Despite the tension, they all enjoyed a hasty breakfast of buttered toast, eggs, and fried potatoes, aware that this might be the last they would have for quite some time. They all ate silently and packed their leftovers in sacks. Lhana also packed dried toast and fruit for the journey. They would have to buy more supplies as they went on or rely on Pirin to hunt while in the wilderness.

While the others gathered their belongings, Lilae sharpened her dagger. For her, packing was always quick. She had nothing of value. She wore her only trinket of worth around her neck. It was a simple silver necklace with shiny stones around a ruby. Besides that, a sack of clothing and an extra pair of boots was all Lilae needed.

Jaiza's grunt sounded like exasperation as she stuffed her favorite dress into her travel bag. She reached for her bow and arrows and headed toward the door, not even looking at Lilae as she passed by.

Once everyone was ready, Lilae hooded herself and followed the procession into the woods. Soon, the sun would rise, and farmers would tend to their cattle and crops.

Delia led the way as they quietly crossed the village to the path leading east. Always east. She cut through the darkness, taking them from gentle paths directly into the thickness of the woods, where the grass was knee high and the hungry bugs were ready to feast on any exposed skin they could find. They were all used to it by now. It would be just another long, hard journey to a foreign land.

Whenever she saw Delia look into the sky, eyes glowing and staff raised, she imagined that she could actually see the Ancients peering down at them from their homes in the Overworld. When Lilae glanced upward, she saw only stars.

"I am glad we have a moment to speak, Lilae. I've been wondering how you feel, now that you're approaching your eighteenth birthday."

"I feel fine." She stuffed her gloved hands into her pockets to warm them. "I am ready for a new journey. I feel more at peace in the wilderness. No one can be mean to me out here, and no one can hurt me." She shrugged it off and forced a smile Delia's way. She didn't want to complain.

"No one can hurt you, Lilae," Delia said, "unless you let them. Have The Winds spoken to you lately?"

"No, they have been quiet."

"Well. Perhaps it is a good thing. They warn you of danger that even I cannot see."

Lilae nodded. "Yes. I don't need The Winds to tell to look out for boys. I'm glad to be free of Jameson's taunting."

"Tell me about this boy."

"He smells like the pigs and always tries to wrestle me in the pits." Lilae scrunched up her nose. "I won't wrestle him, even if I want to twist his arm off."

Delia chuckled softly as she glanced at her. "I'm glad to hear it. I hope you know he wants more than to wrestle, Lilae. I'm sure he fancied you."

"Gross."

"Risa and Jaiza enjoy the company of boys. I'm sure they are ready for marriage, but you know you're different, right?"

"I know. I guess I don't care about the same things that they do. I do not care about friends or boys or starting a family of my own."

A small smile formed on Delia's lips. "Of course not..." She winked at Lilae. "—you're too young to think of such things."

"Am I?" She couldn't see a boy falling in love with her or raising children of her own. But that didn't mean she wouldn't like an adoring, handsome boy professing his love to her; she just didn't think that it was possible. She looked odd. She acted differently. It was better not to dream about such things.

"Don't most girls get married at my age?" She stepped over a fallen tree and waited for the others to do the same.

The grass grew taller, nearing their necks. It was covered in ice, making it so sharp that they had to walk through it with caution. So many years of walking, of moving. When would they stop?

"Sure, some do. There are scores of young girls who, at the first sign of womanhood, begin bearing children, too. And they will do so continuously until the seed no longer catches. But that's not the life for you. You have a future, Lilae. There's a bigger, more important task for you than just producing babies. You are different."

"How? Why? Because there's something wrong with me?"

"No!" Delia waved a flippant hand and peered at Lilae. "Nonsense. There's nothing wrong with you. You're special. You have a very important destiny."

"But why, Delia?" For as long as she could remember, she just went with whatever Delia or Pirin said was best. "How am I special? Why am I being hunted? I've never hurt anyone innocent. I have killed, but I follow the judgment of The Winds."

Delia was silent for a moment. "Soon," she said and patted Lilae on the shoulder.

"She is ready," Lilae heard Delia whisper to herself, as if praying to the Ancients above.

WEEKS HAD PASSED SINCE Lilae and the others had seen another village. They kept off the worn paths and stayed as close to The Barrier as possible. The massive stone structure stood as a constant reminder that they were far from civilization. No one ventured near The Barrier; it was feared.

As they climbed over foothills and through mountain passes, Lilae glanced at the top of The Barrier, where a green haze rippled from the top of the stone to the clouds. She hoped that she'd catch a glimpse of a Silver Elf. Silver Elves shared a wall with the humans, and, in her mind, they were the friendliest of the six remaining races.

The terrain changed from treacherous mountains and valleys, where the snow and wind whipped past their nearly frozen faces, to smooth plains and dense forests. It was like a dream to see the different landforms of Eura.

They crossed over a bridge that connected two massive mountains. When they reached the top, it felt as if they were in the clouds. Whenever Lilae had the nerve to look down, all she saw was a white mist that resembled smoke. Though she couldn't see it, she knew that a river rushed through the valley below. Its waters crashed along the rocks, causing a deafening roar to fill the valley.

Too high, Lilae thought. The wind whipped around her, making her red hair fly into her eyes.

Lilae gulped and tried to catch her breath. Her hands started to shake as she imagined herself plummeting to her death. She hoped the bridge was sturdy enough to support them. Her hands gripped the rough ropes that served as railings so tightly that they cut into the palms of her hands.

Lilae was usually at the head of the pack, but now, she was the last to gather the nerve to cross. She willed herself to move her feet, forcing her mind to stop feeding her images of falling and hitting her head on every rock that lay below.

Her breath sped up. The slats of the bridge were cracking; some were already missing. She looked to Pirin with terrified eyes.

He seemed too far away. Lilae saw him motion for her to cross.

"You can do it, Lilae," Pirin yelled above the roar of the river below.

Lilae looked down again, the mist curling up around her ankles.

"Just take your time."

His patience with her gave her courage. She nodded, more to convince herself that she was ready than anything else.

Lilae took a deep breath and headed toward Pirin. She would hate for him to think of her as a coward. She walked carefully across, praying the entire time. She drew a breath of relief when she safely reached the other side and joined the others.

They began down a steep trail that led back into the wilderness. They were all tired. Everyone was moody. Risa and Jaiza stayed close to each other, as always, and looked simply miserable.

Lilae walked ahead of them all, trapped in her thoughts, clinging to her more pleasant dreams to keep her going. Hunger nagged at her stomach. Her feet were callused and sore from hundreds of miles of walking. Still, she refused to complain.

Pirin once told her that complaints and excuses were signs of weakness. From as early as she could remember, his words were like law, and she lived by his and Delia's teachings.

"Please, Pirin." Lhana stopped abruptly. She breathed heavily, coughing from the cold in the air. She dropped her bags onto the ground with a thud and folded her arms across her chest. "We have been walking since dawn and without a decent break. I am exhausted." Her shoulders slumped. "Please, darling, can we rest now?"

Pirin gave her one look. She was pale, her cheeks red from the wind. There was a small clearing at the mouth of a cavern. He looked to Delia.

The Elder placed her staff in the ground, looked around, and nodded her approval.

That's how it always was: Pirin checking to make sure Delia was in agreement. He shrugged his heavy pack off of his back and held it with one hand.

He nodded toward the cave. Lilae looked at it. It was a small opening in the side of the gray mountain, and all she could see was black inside. She was glad that she wasn't as afraid of the dark as she was of heights.

"This way," Pirin said, leading them to the clearing. They climbed the rocks and heaved their sacks inside the shelter. "This will suffice for the night."

There was a collective sigh of relief and everyone busied themselves with setting up camp inside the hollow mouth of the cave. They would make it as comfortable as possible.

"Looks like rain anyway," Pirin said and peered into the night sky. He sniffed the air. "I'm sure of it. Build a fire inside the cave and we'll sleep there."

"How long can we stay?" Lhana wrapped her arms around his waist.

Pirin looked at Risa. "Until morning."

Jaiza's gaze went to the dark woods on the other side of the cave. "But what about wolves? I saw at least three carcasses on the way up here."

"We'll make a fire. Don't worry," Pirin assured her. "Lilae, go out and place the rabbit traps."

Lilae nodded, uncaring about the cold; it never affected her as it did the others. She wanted to talk further with Delia. Their nights beside the fire, learning and hearing stories, were what Lilae looked forward to each day.

"Who will keep watch?" Jaiza eyed the dark cave and then the forest again. If there was one thing that Jaiza was afraid of, it was wolves.

Pirin had already started to gather wood from fallen branches around the camp. "I'll watch for half of the night, and then you girls can take turns. We'll get horses from the next village and I promise we can stay at an inn."

The twins smiled. Lilae watched their faces light up, and it brought a small smile to her lips. The thought of sleeping in an inn excited them all. There, they could drink ale and meet new people. The food was always hearty, even if the beds were sometimes infested with bed bugs.

Lilae lingered near the slope into the woods while the others set up. She heard something. Her head tilted as she listened to The Winds.

Delia looked back at her, concern spreading across her face. "What is it, Lilae?"

Lilae held a gloved hand up and continued to listen. The Winds spoke to her. They were always there like an old friend. The voices that floated along the breeze or rushing winds always warned her when something was amiss. She had relied on them since she was a child, and they never lied.

Now, they issued a warning.

"Bandits," Lilae said, standing tall. Her eyes searched for movement in the bushes.

"Oh, great. She's talking to herself again," Risa whispered.

"Shush, Risa." Jaiza nudged her sister's arm. "She may talk to herself, but has she ever been wrong?"

Risa didn't reply. They both watched as Lilae stood near the edge of the woods.

"Murderers." The Winds were sure to tell Lilae that, and she gave the twins a look that they understood.

"They followed our tracks, and they wish to rob and kill us." Lilae said it as if she was discussing the weather.

"Humph. I wish they'd try," Jaiza said with a glower in the same direction as Lilae's gaze.

Delia drew in a deep breath. "Holy Elahe. We can never travel in peace?" She stabbed her staff into the ground. "Those bandits are damned fools to be this close to The Barrier."

"I don't like this." Lhana's eyes darted toward the forest as she withdrew to hide near the cave. "Why does this always happen? One day they'll sneak up on us, I just know it!"

"I won't let that happen," Lilae said, glancing back at her.

"You will be the death of me," Lhana said as she turned her back on Lilae.

Pirin gave her a sidelong glance. "Perhaps you'd let me train you sometime, Lhana. You are not as defenseless as you pretend to be. Your trait is quite rare—it could be of use to us."

Lhana glared at him. "I don't want to hear it. You seem to forget that I am a proper lady. Only warriors use their traits."

Pirin shrugged. "Suit yourself. I don't understand why you'd rather waste something you've inherited."

Lhana shook her head. "Never. So stop asking me." She raised a finger. "The first queen of the black throne gave my family my dowry. Who else can make such a claim?"

Risa sighed and gave Jaiza a look. They both set their things down without a word. They'd trained with Lilae for times such as this since they were all children; and this wouldn't be the first group of bandits to threaten them.

Jaiza grabbed her bow, securing her quiver of arrows onto her back.

Risa drew her sword quietly and put the scabbard down. She rolled her shoulders, as if loosening her muscles.

Lilae grinned, her teeth shining in the moonlight. She loved when the twins were like this.

Jaiza stepped beside Lilae, who was younger yet taller. Her keen eyes looked into the growing darkness. "I'll go ahead and see how many there are." She twisted her blonde hair into a knot at the top of her head to keep it from getting in the way.

"There are eight."

"You know everything, don't you?" Jaiza rolled her eyes. "Fine. I can take them out."

Lilae's grin widened. The thrill of a fight excited her. "I'll be right behind you."

Pirin continued to unpack their supplies, shaking out their wool blankets. "This will be good practice for you girls. It's been awhile since you've had a real fight. Maybe you can practice working as a team this time..."

Risa lowered her sword. "Eight? What a waste of energy."

Pirin gave her a stern look.

"What? I was hoping for at least ten," she said as though it was a sport. "That would have been good practice. I can handle eight on my own." She put her sword away and started to help Lhana prepare the salted pork and beans.

"Risa..."

"Father..." Risa said as she squatted down and pulled out an iron pot. "Lilae and Jaiza can take this one."

"Don't be so cocky. You're not the best fighter in the realm by any stretch of the imagination, so stop acting like you know everything. Even your Evasion can be countered if someone has the right skill. Trust me, killing people isn't a game and should not be taken lightly."

Risa raised a brow. "I know it isn't. But Lilae and Jaiza can handle it. We've done this how many times now? At least seven."

"Never underestimate your enemy, Risa. You never know if those men are as trained as you or better."

"You can't be serious." Risa huffed. "I doubt it. We both know that most bandits are nothing more than boys who can barely hold the weight of their own cheap sword."

"You're not listening, are you?"

"Yes, Father. I get what you're saying. I will try not to be so cocky about it. That better?"

Pirin sighed. "You girls are impossible," he said, though a small smile played across his lips.

"You didn't train us to be warriors for nothing," Risa said, as Jaiza slunk into the forest.

Without a sound, Jaiza climbed into a tall tree and disappeared into the branches and leaves.

Lilae stepped out of her cloak with her dagger sharpened and ready in one hand. It was warm on her palm and pulsed for action. She listened to The Winds as they led her to the men who approached her family's camp, careful not to crunch any of the fallen branches beneath her feet.

As the sun's last light faded, she peered silently at the bandits from her place behind a tall oak tree. Energy flowed within her body, and there was an anxiousness filling her throat, and a fire within her veins.

The Winds warned her that the men were merciless. They preyed on innocent travelers, robbing and killing even defenseless women. In return, Lilae and Jaiza would show no mercy.

There was a sudden whistling sound as Jaiza's arrow cut through the dark forest and slammed into the chest of the leader. He gasped loudly, clutching his chest as he was thrown back onto the ground with a solid thud. The arrow was made of the strongest wood and impaled him to the dirt so that he couldn't lift himself.

Lilae noted the look of shock and pain on his face as he strained against the arrow. That look always interested her. It was the look of one surprised by death's touch.

Shouts and frantic orders ensued from the other bandits as they drew their weapons and searched for the source of the arrow. They held their weapons but ducked and cowered toward the safety of the dense, dark forest.

Lilae watched them in silence. She could feel their fear, knowing their hearts were thumping with terror of the unknown. She wanted them to feel that fear. It was the same fear countless others had felt when those men harmed them.

Risa was right about one thing: their weapons were cheap. But these were not boys; they were men who had done this countless times, with success. This would be their last.

"Who's there?" someone shouted in a high-pitched voice that cracked with his words.

"Demons!" another wailed.

"Shut up, Gred. There ain't no stupid demons in this forest!" Lilae heard someone reply, yet she could hear the fear in his voice as if he were uncertain about his own reassurances.

"I told you we shouldn't tempt the Ancients! We're too close to The Barrier!"

Lilae worked quickly, hoping to get some action before Jaiza killed them all with her skilled archery. She took a deep breath, and her vision changed. She could see their moves before they even did them. Everything stilled for her; all sounds muted, and Lilae activated her Focus.

Silence welcome Lilae as she raced into the battle, calculating their every action.

She darted into the mob with her dagger in her fist. She sliced Gred down before he even saw her coming. Lilae didn't waste time making sure he was dead. Her dagger had cut his throat with such precision that there were no doubts.

She slammed into a tall, burly man who seemed more like a solid tree. His body was made of pure muscle, hard as stone. Lilae climbed his body and stabbed him in the neck. Blood spurted into the air.

As he fell backward, his hands racing to cover his wound, she hopped from his body and went on to the next. She didn't need to look back; Lilae always struck true. She could hear him gasping for breath.

Someone grabbed Lilae by her hair from behind. She used her Evasion. Her image flickered before his eyes, and, in an instant, she yanked herself free from his grasp. She kicked him in the back with such force that she heard his spine crack.

His scream resonated throughout the woods, and Lilae put him out of his misery, pouncing onto his back. Her hands were secure against his thick, coarse beard as she snapped his neck.

She stood and turned around. The remaining men were lying on the ground, covered in blood and dirt. Jaiza's arrows protruded from their bodies. Lilae calmed her breathing.

She stood at the center of the massacre. Her eyes closed as she listened to the last groans of pain and gurgles of blood coming from the bandits' mouths. Her Focus subsided, and her vision of the world returned to normal.

Lilae waited until their sounds of dying ceased before making her way back to the camp. She emerged from the forest, her hands and clothes covered in blood splatters. She wiped her face free of a few speckles with a rag that Risa handed her.

Everyone stared at Lilae across the dancing flames as she warmed her bloodstained hands over the burning logs. Her pale face was streaked with blood, and her eyes watched the fire without a trace of emotion.

THE RAIN POURED OUTSIDE the mouth of the cave. Its song was soothing, dripping steadily onto the stones. Lilae enjoyed such private moments with Delia. While the twins had their mother, Lilae had Delia. She still wondered why Lhana had shed that tear earlier. She sensed a deep sadness hidden within that woman.

Lilae sighed, snuggling closer to Delia with her wool blanket. Lilae rested her head on Delia's soft shoulder. She always smelled like mint from the oils she used.

Lilae broke the silence. "Why exactly am I different, Delia?" She had been waiting to ask that question for years now. It was always in her mind. From kingdom to kingdom, she never fit in. "Or special, as you say. Even more importantly, Delia, why is someone hunting me? Why would anyone want me dead?"

For as long as she could remember, Delia and Pirin had only told her the same thing: Someone very bad is after you and will stop at nothing to accomplish his task.

Delia looked down at Lilae, as if considering what to tell her first. "They don't necessarily want you dead, Lilae. They want something from you." She sighed at the perplexed look that Lilae knew crossed her face. "I suppose you're ready."

Delia rose to her feet and held a hand out for Lilae. Lilae accepted the help and stood beside her. Delia was a small woman but that never made Lilae respect her any less. She looked on curiously as Delia held her willow staff out toward the mouth of the cave. A ripple of air floated from the staff and spread. A pale blue light connected to the ripples of air. It covered the entire opening of the cave like a sheer film.

The cave grew warm as if the film stood as a door that closed them inside. Lilae shrugged off her blanket and perked to attention.

"Let's go." She headed toward the ripples of air and stepped through.

Lilae hesitated for a moment, and Delia waved her forward. "Come," she whispered.

She could see Delia through the film. She reached a hand out first, and her body turned frigid. It felt as if a million thorns prickled her flesh, and she winced. She saw Delia standing on the other side, waiting patiently.

"Don't be afraid. It only stings for a second. The shield will not harm any of us. It is laced to shock anyone or anything that I have not named to protect. Do not worry."

She took Lilae's hand and pulled the rest of her body through. Delia walked into the darkness of the forest, expecting Lilae to follow. She held her staff before her, leading the way. Lilae was surprised that they walked deeper and deeper into the forest.

The rain stopped but the ground was muddy and squishy beneath their boots. She could barely see ahead of her. She was afraid that they were being watched, yet The Winds were silent.

Lilae held on to Delia's small waist to keep from falling over. They walked for what felt like hours, and Lilae fought to keep her questions to herself. She could feel that it was time. Finally, she would know who she was, and what her future held. They stopped by a body of water.

Lilae stared at the lake, feeling the cold air drift closer to her. The soft patter of drizzle sprinkled onto its surface, bathed in moonlight. Lilae held her hand out, catching a cool droplet of water in her palm. Rain was one of her favorite things in the world. It was cooling and calming.

Delia walked to the edge of the water and waved her closer. "Kneel."

Lilae took off her boots and stepped closer. She loved the feel of the mud on her feet and stepped close enough for the water to lap over her toes. She knelt down beside the lake and looked up at Delia.

"Good. Now bow your head and close your eyes."

Lilae breathed deeply and looked out over the water. She bowed her head, and her eyes fluttered closed. Lilae nearly choked as she was grabbed violently and dragged into the water.

Lilae's eyes popped open as the water slapped her face. All she saw was darkness. Her mouth filled with water; she quickly tried to push the liquid out and close her mouth.

She could hold her breath for only so long, and her entire body froze with fear as something held her hand and pulled her deeper and deeper into the water. Lilae fought the urge to scream. Whatever held on to her was rough and unyielding. She could feel the hate and evil radiating from it. She fought to see ahead of her. She wanted to see what had hold of her, but all she saw before her were the inky depths of the lake.

Her ears filled with fluid, and her eyes began to burn. Two yellow eyes glowed back at her, and Lilae felt her body shake.

She screamed. "Delia!"

Water flooded every orifice, and she panicked. She tried to regain her composure, but those eyes bore into hers. A hand went over her mouth and pressed her face deeper into the water until her head scraped the bottom of the lake.

Lilae flailed and fought. She needed air. Her mind became a torrent of screams and pleas. Her lungs burned. Her nose burned. Her heart thumped so fast that she was sure it would explode. And then, she saw a face. Bronze skin, yellow eyes that glowed beneath the water, and high cheekbones. Terror filled her very bones, creeping into her soul.

"Join me, Lilae. Or die," the creature said in a voice that was unlike anything Lilae had ever heard. It wasn't human; it had to be some sort of a demon from the Underworld.

Lilae shook her head. She felt lightheaded, as if she was dying. Still, she refused.

"No!" She swallowed more water. She reached past the face and toward the surface. She could see light. She craved that light.

"Join me and I will ease your pain."

"No!"

Pain jolted through her body like a flood of hot acid.

"Then, your fate it sealed. You will be mine whether you choose to or not."

Like a slap to the face, Lilae was jolted back to the surface. Delia had her by her shirt's collar. She leaned over Lilae, closely watching for her reaction. Lilae coughed and choked as air flooded into her lungs. Cool, delicious air. She breathed it in greedily. She saw Delia nod with approval and sit back on her heels. She wrapped Lilae in her cloak, giving her a moment to calm down.

"What was that?" Lilae shrieked.

Delia put her hand out. "Quiet your voice."

Lilae shot to her feet, flinging off the cloak. She looked over at the lake. It was still now, peaceful. She would never look at water the same way.

Lilae's face heated, and tears stung her eyes. She had thought that she was going to die under the lake's surface; she never wanted to feel that way again. Lilae looked at Delia as tears slipped down her cheeks. She wiped furiously at them.

"What was that, Delia?"

Delia picked up the cloak off the ground and draped it over Lilae's shoulders. "First, tell me your choice. Did you choose to side with him?

"Who was that?"

"Answer the question, Lilae. It's important!"

Confused, Lilae tried to gather her thoughts. Wiping her face she shook her head. "I told him no."

Delia closed her eyes and let out a breath of relief. "Good girl. There is still hope then." She opened her eyes and pulled Lilae in for a hug.

Lilae buried her face in the warmth of Delia's chest. The comfort of her embrace still didn't banish the fear that threatened to make her cry out in hysterics.

"That was an apparition of the Ancient, Wexcyn. He has returned from his imprisonment in the abyss. He has come to claim his throne. And now, he knows that you cannot be swayed to fight on his side. You have denied him."

Lilae pulled away from Delia. That name did not sound familiar. She shook her head. "I don't understand." Cold water dripped from her clothes. She pulled the cloak closer to warm herself. She shivered and slumped to the ground, resting her back on a smooth cluster of rocks.

Her gaze went back to the water, and her eyes glazed over as she recalled the terror she had just experienced. There was a time when Lilae thought that she feared nothing.

Delia made a fire with the tip of her staff onto a rock. Lilae glanced over her shoulder. Such a fire was not possible, but Delia had a talent for the impossible.

Sitting beside Lilae, Delia put a hand on her shoulder and stroked it tenderly. "I'm sorry, Lilae, but I had to show you. Showing you what evil we are up against is better than just telling you. I find it much more effective."

Lilae scoffed. "It was quite effective, Delia. And it was uncalled for."

"I don't think so, Lilae. Wexcyn is a threat to everything you know and love."

"Was that real?"

"It was." Delia looked up at the stars. "It was real in your mind. I could see nothing of the encounter, but that doesn't mean that it didn't happen. Wexcyn invaded your thoughts. We are lucky that he is not strong enough to actually harm you from a distance. But soon, anything will be possible."

"Who is Wexcyn?"

Delia pulled her journal from her bag. It was a small book made of supple leather and filled with parchment.

It was the book Delia used to teach Lilae ever since Lilae was a child. There were ancient maps, history lessons, illustrations, and prophecies. Delia licked her thumb and flipped through a couple of weathered pages; she held open a page with a map on it. The map was drawn with such precision that Lilae wondered if Delia was an artist and had done it herself.

"You know about the four realms, Lilae, right?"

Lilae nodded. As a child, she had loved to learn and recite what she memorized. It was rare for anyone other than royalty and nobility to even be able to read. "Yes, of course. There's

Eura, the human realm. Alfheim, the Silver Elf realm. Kyril, the Tryan realm. And Nostfar, the Shadow Elf realm."

Delia smiled. She smoothed a wild ringlet of Lilae's hair behind her ear. "Good girl. And who created the races?"

"Delia, we have traveled for as long as I can remember, and I've never heard anyone even mention the other races. Why is that?"

"Because it has been so long since anyone has seen someone from another race that it simply isn't thought about anymore. Can you tell me who created the remaining races?"

"Pyrii created the Tryans, Inora created the Shadow Elves, Ulsia the Silver Elves, and Telryd created the humans." Then, Lilae lifted an eyebrow. "You said... the remaining races. There were others?"

"Yes. Lord Elahe, the creator of the entire universe, created many Ancients to start new worlds... But we'll get to that another day. I am afraid I don't have time to explain the origins of the universe quite yet."

"But the others?" Lilae persisted. "What happened to them?"

Delia pointed to the lines that separated each realm from one another.

"The Barriers," she explained, "were created by the Ancients to keep us from warring with each other. When they created the different races, it was glorious. First, there was peace, and they were pleased. However, everything changed... when death was discovered. With the first death, the perfect world they had created and loved started to crumble. Quests for power and greed took over. Evil was born, and it infected some of the Ancients as well. Things were so bad when all of the races lived together that they almost destroyed our world." Delia turned the page to a picture of the Ancients.

"The Ancients created The Barriers to keep us safe from one another's powers, to return the world to balance."

Lilae examined the drawing of the Ancients.

Delia pointed to a picture of what resembled a man, except he seemed to be made of some type of metal.

He sat on a dark throne with a long spear in his hand and an intense look on his bronze face. Even as a picture, he seemed to stare back at Lilae, looking into her soul. She shivered and turned her eyes to the fire, scooting closer to Delia for warmth and protection. Before that night, Lilae thought that she feared nothing; she now feared Wexcyn with every fiber of her being.

"Wexcyn was the first Ancient created by Elahe. He was so powerful that his creations were able to manipulate any power that the other races could. He was almost too powerful, and he knew it. He wanted to rule his brothers and sisters. He wanted to be God."

"What Ancient was he, Delia? Who were his people?"

"They were called Mithrani. They were a beautiful race."

"And now they are all gone?"

"After the war, they hid. They are out there... Somewhere. And he was imprisoned in the abyss for his crimes. Wexcyn started an alliance with a few of the other Ancients. What they did in the Great War changed everything. They discovered something that threatened the entire world."

Lilae sat up straighter. She could picture everything Delia spoke of. The races, the gods, the war. "What happened? What did they change?"

"They discovered that each death of an individual makes their Ancient weaker."

Lilae nodded. "It makes sense," she said and ran a finger across her bottom lip as she thought. "Delia... the Great War wasn't about us, was it? It was really a fight between the Ancients?"

"Indeed."

Lilae stared at the picture again. Those eyes would haunt her until the day she died. He had once been the most powerful Ancient in existence. What would he do to her if he was close enough? He resembled a human, yet he seemed to be a supernaturally enhanced version. Seeing him hold that golden spear worried her. She could picture that spear impaling her.

Lilae furrowed her eyebrows as she looked at his picture. "Is that what is coming, Delia? Another war?"

"They have already taken sides, my dear. This war has been brewing for ages. I am afraid we can no longer avoid it. The Ancients knew that Wexcyn couldn't stay imprisoned forever. He has too many supporters who have been trying to free him for centuries."

Lilae looked at the sky, imagining as she always did that she could see the Ancients up there in the Overworld. "And who is on our side, Delia?"

"The odds are in our favor... for now. Telryd, Ulsia, and Pyrii fight for life, for the preservation of this world."

"So that leaves Inora, the Shadow Elves' Ancient. She betrayed us, then."

"I wish it were that easy, Lilae. I really do. I fear the other Ancients have returned, as well. There are races that you've never even heard of, hiding out there... ready for revenge."

"Bellens, you mean?"

"Where did you hear that word?"

"I overhead a woman in Sabron say something about them to a little girl. She told the girl that if she didn't do her chores, a Bellen would come and eat her."

Delia signed. "Damned idiot, whoever that woman was."

Lilae folded her arms across her chest and held her blanket tightly. She had waited so long to hear this story, and yet, something told her that she was already a part of it all. "That's what you meant though, right?"

"Yes. As we speak, they prepare for war in my home. They have made the Underworld into something it was never meant to be. The Underworld was supposed to be a place for the dead to reconnect with their lost loved ones, and go to their last home." Delia looked off then, and Lilae felt badly. She couldn't help but forget that Delia was not of this world. Her home had already been taken, and now she hoped to help Lilae keep hers. "I escaped when Wexcyn killed my brothers and sisters. I was aided by the Ancients, so that I could take you before someone else did."

Lilae rested her head against Delia's shoulder again. She scratched at a mosquito bite. "Tell me, Delia. Where do I fit into all of this? Why did you take me?"

Delia stroked Lilae's hair. "Lilae, you are a remarkable young woman. Do you know that?"

Lilae half smiled as she watched the fire. She didn't want Delia to keep anything from her anymore, so she tried to look as if she were brave. "No more stalling, Delia. Go on—tell me. Am I an Ancient or something?" she joked.

Delia didn't say anything. Instead, she pulled back and stared at Lilae. "What did you say?"

Lilae sat up straight. "What? I was joking."

Delia's face was paler than Lilae had ever seen it. She narrowed her eyes at Lilae so that only a small glow replaced her irises. Lilae shuddered. "What is it?"

Delia shook her head. "Lilae, I don't know what possessed you to say that. You are too smart for your own good."

"You're not saying..."

Delia shook her head and waved her hands. "No. No, you're not an Ancient."

Lilae sighed in relief. "That's a relief." Her shoulders slumped. "What then?"

"You were close though, my dear. You are of the Chosen class. With the end of the Great War, the losing Ancients fled, and Wexcyn, the leader, was imprisoned. As a truce, The Barriers were created. However, the truce said that one day another war would be fought... This time for total domination. But here is the thing, Lilae. It was agreed that each race would produce an heir of the Ancients. You are Telryd's heir."

"How is such a thing possible?"

Delia sat up and leaned a little closer to Lilae, her tone rushing with excitement. "The truce states that the fate of the world would be put in the hands of the people. The Ancients are letting their creations decide who will lead in the Overworld, and there will be no further disputes. They all agreed. It is set in stone. You are the one they call the Flame. You were chosen to lead the humans in this war."

Lilae folded her legs and looked over her shoulder again, feeling as though someone watched her from the dark forest.

"You're saying that I will fight Shadow Elves, all to keep Telryd's place secure in the Overworld? Why can't he fight for himself?"

"Lilae, if an Ancient stepped into this world, the balance of power would shift, and the world would not be the same. There's no telling what damage would be done. It must be done by the races."

Lilae squeezed her eyes shut and touched her temples with her fingertips. Her head throbbed. There was just too much to process. "What do I have to do?"

"You will lead the humans against Wexcyn and the forgotten races, and we will hope for the best. For, if you fail, there will be new leadership in the Overworld. Do you understand what that would mean?"

"There would be no more humans."

"Exactly. There would be no more humans, Silver Elves, or Tryans. Shadow Elves will thrive, and Wexcyn will re-create his fallen race." Delia sat back and pulled her cloak tighter. The air grew colder, and the wind picked up speed. "Those of the Chosen class are all named. You are the Flame, there is also the Storm, the Inquisitor, the Seer, the Steel, and the last is the Cursed. He will be Wexcyn's greatest weapon."

Lilae sighed. "Delia, this is too much." She was having a hard time keeping up a brave front.

"I know that this is a tough fate to accept." Delia leaned back. "I really thought you were ready. I have no choice but to tell you all that I can. Soon, we might not have an opportunity to talk about these things. We must prepare. The Storm is already heading this way. You have to be ready for his arrival. He will be the closet to you, for Pyrii and Telryd are like brothers. Tryans have always been great friends to the humans. As for the other Chosen, they have been ready for years now. We all have been waiting for you."

Lilae stared at the fire. The flames were dying down. She had an odd urge to touch them. Somehow, she knew she could do it. She almost reached out but resisted. She sighed and gazed sidelong at Delia.

"But..." She cleared her throat and tried to straighten her back. "What if I don't want to? Will they replace me? If I am too afraid... can I choose my own path?" Delia shot her a look that made her face pale. She immediately felt embarrassed by her question and looked away.

Delia folded her hands on her lap. "Lilae, dear, I know this must be very hard for you. I've studied human emotion for centuries, and while I do not have such feelings, I am empathetic. But my duty is to see the bigger picture. This entire thing is about more than just you. However, you are the one who must do it. We have waited for someone to be born with all of the necessary power. That someone is you. There will be no replacements."

Lilae looked down at her hands. Delia couldn't understand how she was feeling. She wasn't human and never would be. She was a supernatural being in human flesh. Could Delia even love her? It hurt to think that she was just business to Delia.

Delia noticed the look in Lilae's eyes. She put a hand on Lilae's. "You are strong, Lilae. You can do this."

So, there are five others out there just like me. I wonder if they are as miserable with this burning power as I am. Somehow, she couldn't tell Delia that she had been feeling stranger than normal lately, that she could feel the power that

Delia was telling her about. It kept her awake at night, begging to be released.

"I'm afraid, Delia." She avoided eye contact with the Elder. She said it calmly, but she could feel the fear rising in her throat, making her almost giddy. "Is that normal?"

"It's the most normal emotion of them all, my dear."

Lilae pulled her blankets closer. "At least that part of me is human enough." She stared up at the stars, listening to the fire crackle.

"Good girl." Delia smiled and kissed her forehead. "You are the best choice the Ancients could have made, and one day, you'll understand why."

Lilae smiled. She felt comforted by Delia's kiss. Such affection was so rare from her.

Delia stood. "Let's return to camp before the others wake up."

Lilae nodded and followed her back through the forest. When they returned, everyone was still asleep. Delia kept the shield up and put her bedroll beside the fire. She leaned her staff against the wall and watched Lilae as she stood staring past the shield into the darkness.

"Get some rest, Lilae. We will be reaching new territory soon enough." Delia moved away from the fire and pulled her blanket over her. "Soon," Delia said, and smiled at her warmly, "you'll see a real spring."

Lilae nodded absently and grabbed her pack.

"Good night, Delia." She sat down and looked into the fire. She had so much information to process. Lilae always knew she was different, but now that she finally started to realize what was brewing inside, it frightened her.

She looked over her shoulder and into the woods. The quiet all around her made the hairs on her arm stand on end just thinking that Wexcyn was there, watching her. She lay on her bedroll and folded her arms across her chest as her mind drifted, wondering if the other chosen ones were as afraid as she was.

"I KNOW WHAT YOU'RE AFRAID OF, my love," Sona whispered into Liam's ear.

Liam grinned and closed his eyes. She was the only one welcome to disturb his solitude. Sona kissed the back of his neck and ran her fingers through his hair. She smelled of lavender and honey. He caught her in his arms. She was light in his grasp and smiled up at him.

"And what is that?" Liam leaned in to kiss her on the lips. They were as soft as rose petals and similarly colored.

"Our wedding night." Sona giggled, and he showered her with passionate kisses all over her white throat. "You're afraid you won't know what to do with me." She wrapped her arms around his neck as he grabbed her skirts into a bunch, pressing her against the mantle of the fireplace.

He lifted her by the thighs. She wrapped them around his waist and let his hands slide up her stockings. "I'm sure I'll figure it out," he whispered, as his hand caressed her smooth legs.

"Prince Liam!" a shrill voice called.

Liam sighed, resting his forehead against Sona's. She looked up at him with the most unsettling blue eyes he'd ever seen.

"That woman," Sona growled under her breath. "Does she follow you everywhere?"

Liam agreed with the sentiment; he never got a moment's peace. There was always something to do, somewhere to be, for as long as he could remember.

"What?" Liam couldn't mask the irritation in his voice. He rolled his eyes as he heard the high-heeled footsteps enter the room. He knew those clicks along the floor all too well.

Lady Cardelia stepped into the quiet room. Liam quickly put Sona back onto the floor and straightened his clothing. His tutor frowned as she looked at the both of them. Her glare lingered on Sona in particular.

Lady Cardelia's serious blue eyes lifted to Liam's face. Her spectacles made her eyes look even bigger as she regarded him. He remembered when he used to draw caricatures of her during their lessons. He also remembered being struck across his hands with a stick whenever she caught him.

"Queen Aria asked me to find you. It is your birthday ball, after all." Lady Cardelia spoke slowly, precisely, always proper and composed. "You have guests, Prince Liam. You shouldn't spend the entire night hiding."

Liam gave a nod, even though he cared nothing about being paraded for guests he didn't know. "I'm coming."

"And you, Lady Sonalese Rochfort—" She shot a raptor-like glare at Sona. "What would Lord Rochfort think if he knew you were back here without a chaperone, with your dress gathered up around your waist? That is not ladylike at all."

Sona looked back at her. Her blue eyes held an icy glare. "I dare you to speak one word to my father."

Liam watched as Sona walked directly up to Lady Cardelia. He once thought that Lady Cardelia was one of the most intimidating women he had ever seen; that was, until he met Sona. The young woman fluffed out her petticoats and indigo skirts and retied her white bow around her tiny waist.

Sona was a noblewoman. Her father, Lord Rochfort, owned all of Klimmerick's Row, the wealthiest street of row houses and shops in Oren. He was a prominent political figure, and yet Sona didn't care about the constraints her title should have put on her. Sona did what she wanted. Liam envied her. Perhaps that was why he had proposed to her.

"But, haven't you heard that I am going to be your queen one day... Lady Longneck?" Sona grinned evilly at the look of shock on Lady Cardelia's face. "That is what everyone calls you."

Liam dared to look at Lady Cardelia. The tension in the room was stifling. Sona never censored her speech; she said whatever was on her mind. Lady Cardelia's face turned red.

Sona began to leave the room. She glanced back at the wiry older woman whose ruffled collar was buttoned all the way up to beneath her chin. Liam's brows lifted. Lady Cardelia almost seemed to shrink under Sona's glare.

Impressive, Liam thought. No one can make that woman as much as flinch.

"I don't care what you tell him. He'd probably have you killed anyway," she said with a flippant shrug of her shoulders, "for spreading such vicious lies." She grabbed her silk shawl from the back of a mahogany chair then flashed a smile at Liam. "I'll see you later, darling." She waved graciously and disappeared into the crowd outside the door as if nothing had happened.

Liam stood there silently as Lady Cardelia waited. He almost rolled his eyes when she lifted a long thin finger to wiggle at him. He knew the scolding was about to begin.

"Liam." Lady Cardelia looked to him.

Liam raised an eyebrow. "Prince Liam to you," he said.

She put her hands on her hips and gave him her best scowl. "Oh, don't try that with me, Liam. I've been your tutor since you were a little wild toddler wetting your pants. Don't give me any sass. That girl you're marrying may have a filthy tongue, but you know better."

Liam sighed. No point arguing.

She shook her head, her face softening. "Why are you hiding in here, Liam?" Her voice came out much gentler that time.

Liam shrugged, glancing at the doorway. Too many people. Outside those doors were thousands of people waiting to see him. They were crowded in all of the public rooms of the Orenian castle. So many people made him nervous.

She offered a small smile. "You're twenty-five years old today, Liam. You cannot hide anymore. All of those people out there are expecting you to protect the kingdom. No masks or disguises can hide you now. Your time has come."

Liam put his hands in his pockets. He swallowed. She was right. It was time. This would be the last night that he would be in the castle. For years, he'd thought he wanted nothing more than to escape his studies and see what the real world had to offer; and now, the time had come, and only he knew just what that meant. Being a scholar brought more than knowledge.

He'd studied the prophecies. He knew what was coming.

"I know, Lady Cardelia. We've prepared for years now. I am ready," he said, standing just a little taller. He tried to give a reassuring smile.

Liam knew she already doubted him in her head. Many of his subjects looked at him with skepticism. This was supposed to be our savior? He could read that very question in their eyes. He wasn't a big man or remarkably tall. He was too skinny compared to his warrior friends. Liam feared that he was too... ordinary to be someone special.

He started toward the door and she caught him by the wrist. "Prince Liam, listen for a moment."

He lifted a brow. Her face looked troubled.

"I know you're leaving tomorrow and everything, but promise me something."

Liam nodded. "What is it?" He wanted to make his way to his private quarters. He wanted to get a good night's rest before he left with the Order of Oren. His friends would be ready and waiting for him in the morning.

Lady Cardelia's eyes were wet with tears. It made Liam uncomfortable. She had always been the strictest of tutors. He didn't like seeing her façade fade.

"Don't let anything you see out there in the wild lands change you. Don't let anyone taint your good heart, especially that foul woman who dares to call herself a lady."

"Watch yourself. Lady Rochfort is my fiancée."

She shook her head. "I'm sorry, but I don't know how you chose her out of every lovely young woman at court. She isn't good enough for you."

He turned away from her. Why wasn't she being fair about Sona? Sona never did anything to hurt anyone.

"She loves me," Liam replied. "And who says I'm good enough for any of those women outside those doors?"

"You speak as if you are incapable of being loved. We all love you, Liam. There is no need to settle. Most of those people out there have no idea what you really are, but I know. You fight for our entire race. Stay focused, and don't let us down."

She had never spoken this way. Her words worried him. "I promise." He left her in the empty cloakroom and entered the busy hallway. It was after midnight, and the ball was still in full swing.

He walked with his hands in his pockets, and then remembered Lord Eisenmoore's gentleman's training and quickly took them out. While Lady Cardelia had spent years training him to be a scholar, Lord Eisenmoore had tried his best to train Liam to be the perfect gentleman, the future king. Still, he forgot some things at times.

"Prince Liam," the guests said whenever he passed. They bowed and glanced at him in awe. Sixteen years secluded in the vaults, and nine more spent in the walls of the military stronghold in the north, and none of his civilian subjects had ever seen his face, until tonight.

Liam nodded to each of those who addressed him. Though he walked with his back straight and his face calm, inside he was a ball of nerves and nausea for being stared at so. His black hair had been brushed and styled differently than any man who attended the ball.

"A future king must set the trends," Lord Eisenmoore said, "not follow them." Tomorrow, most of the men in court would try to sport the same hairstyle.

Liam wore a rich red-and-white tailored suit and walked with his jewel-encrusted sword at his hip. There was a time when a weapon felt foreign to him, but after being locked away with the other soldiers of the elite Order of Oren, he was never without his sword again. It was an extension of him now, and he wielded it with an expertise that couldn't be explained in someone so young.

Faces: smiling faces, judging faces, envious faces, adoring faces. So many faces, and he didn't recognize any of them. He wished his best friend, Rowe, were a nobleman. He wished the captain had been allowed to come. Instead, he was forced to mingle with complete strangers, people who probably secretly wanted him to fail.

Liam was the only heir, and there were those who wanted him dead. There were fools who coveted the throne. They still went about their political intrigues and scheming as if everything was the same. They had no idea what was coming to their realm.

Liam avoided the stares and looked up at his mother. Queen Aria seemed to glow a little brighter than the other Tryans around her.

This was Kyril, realm of the Tryans and the fairies. Every Tryan had a glow that reached from the inside out, and yet she stood out as if a light shone only for her. He felt a lump in his throat. Her piercing gaze rested on him, and she smiled. This might be his last night seeing her beautiful face, and in an instant, he could see that same thought reflected in her eyes.

Oh, mother, he thought. Stop reading my mind!

She grinned. It was a secret smile, and only Liam knew its meaning. Forgive me, it is a terrible habit, she said silently back to him.

Liam walked up the short staircase to the row of thrones. There were only two, when there had once been three. His father had been dead for twenty years now, and he still remembered where he used to sit up there.

"Liam, my boy," Queen Aria said and hugged him.

Liam stood beside her, and there was a loud cheer from the crowd. She raised his hand up with hers and smiled down at the large ballroom packed with Tryans dressed in their absolute best finery.

"Tonight," she called, "my son salutes you all, for he is the chosen one who will deliver us from the hands of evil. These are indeed dark times. He will rid our realm of the murderous Shadow Elf clans that invade our territory. He will protect us."

The crowd cheered even louder. Liam almost wanted to shout at them. They knew nothing. Shadow Elves weren't nearly as bad as what they really should fear. As Queen Aria smiled at the crowd, she locked arms with Liam.

Liam, I love you, she said silently to him. Even while she smiled at her people, Liam could feel the tension. I've tried to protect you for as long as I could, but I fear The Barriers are being opened. We both know there are more sinister things in the works. We both know that Wexcyn wants you dead. She looked at him, worry lines tainting her forehead. She gave his hand a squeeze. Please, don't get yourself killed out there. Get the talisman from the Alden clan in Raeden and wait for my word. I fear the time to meet the others is upon us.

Liam nodded. Do not worry mother, Liam thought. His mother could read most anyone's mind; his was not immune. The Alden clan will willingly give us the talisman for safekeeping. And as far as the Shadow Elves are concerned... They don't know the havoc I will unleash upon them.

He could feel his adrenaline start to rush. The time for reading books and scrolls was over. The time for training and preparing had come to an end. He thumbed his hilt. Tomorrow, his sword would taste blood, and there would be no turning back.

LIAM TILTED HIS HEAD and listened to The Winds as they whispered to him.

They're coming for you, they warned.

"What?" Without a reply, they faded with the crisp breeze.

Liam looked to the dull, gray sky. Dew clung to the thin overhanging branches and the mountain air smelled sweet. It was just before dusk—when the Shadow Elves would awaken for their nocturnal activities—and Liam was ready for battle. He sat tall above his black horse, waiting for the right moment to attack the Shadow Elves below.

Liam patted Midnight, his battle horse, and smoothed his hind leg. He leaned forward and spoke in a hushed tone to the horse. "Are you ready?"

Midnight neighed in reply and kicked his legs.

Liam waved a hand and motioned for the troupe of soldiers behind him to move closer. There were about a hundred Tryan soldiers waiting for his command. They looked around at the empty space before them and the long drop beneath them. Still, Liam had their complete trust.

Liam held the reigns tight in his grip and took a deep breath. The cool air entered his lungs, and he closed his eyes. He focused on his power, the energy that flowed within his veins. The clouds began to move closer together, creating a tight knit form in the sky that completely blocked the sun. When Liam opened his eyes, they were no longer blue. They were as black as night.

The Tryans behind him were unafraid. They were the elite warriors of the Order of Oren. Liam had been locked away with these men and women for nearly ten years. He had trained with them and lived with them as an equal.

Commoners like Rowe and nobles like Sona, none of that mattered in the Order. This group was like family, and they would follow him into the Underworld, if necessary. They waited for Liam to signal them. One hand clutched the reins of their horses, the other on the hilts of their swords.

Liam raised his large jewel-encrusted sword into the air with a loud cry and urged Midnight on. Midnight jumped, and over the cliff they went. Liam held tight. His eyes narrowed fiercely, and his sword began to glow white in the darkness. The horse's hooves searched for footing and found none.

Thunder cracked loudly above them, as if the sky was about to break open and fall upon them with rage. Liam sucked in a breath of the cool air and lightning shot across the sky. Liam caught the light in his sword and directed it beneath them, making a pathway of blinding light so that his men could file steadily behind him.

The horses' hooves sparked along the road of lightning, a shrill sound deafening the soldiers as they slid toward the ground. The valley led them directly to the camp of Shadow Elves.

The effect was perfect, so perfect that Liam couldn't help but crack a smile. Liam wanted it to look as though he and his men were coming straight from the sky. The Shadow Elves woke with a start at the noise as an army of horses jumped from the path of lightning and trampled into the rocky valley. The vibrations shook the terrain, and their enemy was frozen with obvious terror. In an instant, the battle began.

A swarm of Shadow Elves scrambled from their tents. They moved with such speed that their figures were barely traceable. However, Tryan eyes were equipped to spot them. Even though they darted in and out of the shadows, they couldn't hide.

The Shadow Elves hissed like snakes when they saw the royal colors of the Oren palace. There was blue and red on their breastplates and armor. With Liam leading them, it made them all the more fearsome.

The Shadow Elves had heard about the prince. Liam was the first male heir in centuries, and his reputation in the field was notorious amongst the invading elves. Ten years in training and smaller battles with rival clans and wildlings had made Liam a force to be reckoned with. His grim expression was illuminated by another flash of lightning. He swung his enchanted sword, and lightning whipped out like a terrifying rope of electric currents. It cut through groups of elves like butter, slaying them by the dozens. The remaining elves began to flee from its path.

Yes, just run away. Liam grinned in triumph as they retreated back to their own barrier. This can end quickly if you just run. And many did run, back to the cruel, dark realm of Nostfar.

The Shadow Elves who remained were quick and agile, with fighting styles that the Orens had never seen. They were like predators, calculating and precise. One leapt from the ground and reached for Liam's sword.

Liam saw him coming and sliced the elf's outstretched hand off. The glow of his sword made the wound sizzle as though it had been stuck with a hot poker. The smell of burning flesh struck Liam's nostrils as the Shadow Elf shrieked in pain and tumbled to the ground.

Before Liam could turn, another was on his back, a blue crystal dagger clutched in its grasp. It never ceased to amaze him how lightning-fast they were; like cats, they pounced and darted. His eyes widened as the blade came toward his face.

He turned his head and grabbed the Shadow Elf by its long black hair, slinging it to the ground with such force that it flew into a nearby tree. Liam's eyes tracked the body, and, with a point of his sword, he sent a flash of light that knocked the Shadow Elf from the branches and onto the hard ground. One more down. Liam grinned as he turned Midnight around and charged headfirst into an oncoming flurry of Shadow Elves with the power of the Ancient Pyrii flowing through his veins.

ROWE CHARGED THROUGH THE MASSES with untamed vigor. His ax hung low at the side of his horse. His pulse quickened as he gripped the heavy ax in his large fist, the bands on the hilt pressing hard into his roughened palm.

Rowe lifted it slightly and, with a grunt, he leaned forward, swinging the ax powerfully into the heads of the surrounding Shadow Elves. A spray of blood filled the air like a fog.

Skin split open and bone crushed beneath his ax. It glowed blue, and he knew that it stung their flesh as it cut through. The yells and noise were deafening, and so was the blood that rushed as his heart pumped with adrenaline.

Rowe's horse wouldn't slow. Like every other horse ridden by a Tryan on the battlefield, his was connected with its rider. Each horse could feel the same, sense their thoughts, and anticipate what the rider wanted. Rowe's veered right and into another group of Shadow Elves that tried to slice the horse's belly or legs, trying anything to get the Tryan soldier to the ground.

Rowe kicked one with his heavy-booted foot and thrust the ax into the neck of another. The glowing blade sliced straight through the soft flesh of its neck and barely paused to cut through the bone. Other elves looked in horror as the head rolled off of its body to the muddy ground.

Rowe sat up and swung the blood from his blade, not stopping as he continued on to the next unfortunate being in his eyesight.

"SONA!" THE TRYAN WOMAN on the white horse heard someone shout her name from beyond the dense cluster of elves she was attacking.

Her head snapped up toward the voice, her hands tight on her horse's reins. Rowe pointed to a tent on the far side of the field.

"There!"

Sona nodded, and her horse instantly understood the orders. They galloped through the crowd as the Shadow Elves continued to fight with the Tryan soldiers on the ground. Sona grinned despite the calamity all around her.

The Shadow Elves reached for her as she passed by, but her horse was too fast for them. She ran them over with such a force that many lay crushed behind.

Once they reached the tent, she hopped from the horse's back. Sona reached both hands over her head and grabbed her dual swords from behind her. The swords glowed blue with her touch, and, with a face of determination, she charged through the tents flaps. Inside, three Shadow Elves crouched over a circular table.

Her large blue eyes widened. The surface of the table was black like smoke, and images of other Shadow Elves flickered along the smoke. The smoke disappeared, and the Shadow Elf captains lunged at her.

"Kill the Tryan!"

With a curved sword in each hand, she crisscrossed them and sliced the first elf straight through his abdomen. With a pull of the swords, she cut him in half. Blood splattered onto the tent's walls as she flung one sword at the elf to her right.

He fell backward with the force of her throw, as the sword lodged into his spine. The screams filled her ears, but she was in a trance. With only one sword, she saw the other elf dart to her like lightning.

Sona grunted as he elbowed her in the face before she could catch him with her sword. She tasted the saltiness of her own blood, and it enraged her. Her eyes narrowed. He may have caught her off guard with his Shadow Walk, but he would only get one hit. She would not make that mistake twice.

Her sword caught the handle of his dagger and tossed it into the air. He growled and ducked as she tried to cut off his head. The glowing sword missed, but she anticipated his move and kicked him in the chin, knocking him backward. She lunged on top of him, her sword's blade pressed against his neck.

"Who sent you?" Sona clenched her teeth as he tried to push her off.

His thin eyes were completely white and matched his tattoos almost perfectly. A smile spread across his face. "Is that a trick question?" he asked with a raised brow and a grin that was meant to taunt Sona.

Sona's gaze bore into his, watching the light fade from his eyes as she pressed the blade into his neck. He wrapped his thin hands around her throat in a desperate attempt to stop her. She closed her eyes and finished the job. His hands fell back to the ground, limp and lifeless.

Sona stood and closed her eyes. Heart thumping, she wiped a streak of the Shadow Elf's blood on both cheeks, readied her swords, and stepped from the tent into the blackness of night that only her fiancé could have arranged on a spring morning.

She saw him on his black horse, regal and full of a confidence he didn't normally display. She watched him as she let the light from her glowing body seep into her swords. A tiny bit of light made them blue. A tiny bit more made them yellow. She shook a bit as she poured nearly all of her light into the swords, and made them red with power.

IN THE DISTANCE, LIAM WATCHED Sona run through the surrounding masses with her swords overenchanted so much that the red glow caused a cloud of smoke to encircle her.

Seeing her in action was like witnessing a tale from the storybooks he'd been read as a child. He was proud of her.

He never doubted any of them, but he could see that some of the men were fighting only to be surprised by the elves' speed. This made them focus even harder and fight with more intensity. Once you had an elf in your sight, you'd better kill them quick, lest they slip through your fingers and stab you in the back.

Liam breathed hard, the adrenaline surging through him. He saw Sona climb onto her horse again, bloodstained but as beautiful as a goddess.

The Tryans had so much to prove to the other races, and Liam was confident that his Order was made up of the perfect warriors for the task.

The fairies were busy keeping track of anyone wounded, ready to heal anyone in need. His reflexes were sharp. He heard the wind swish as a Shadow Elf raced through the crowd and onto the back of Liam's horse. He felt the cold hands reach around his neck, a small blade at his throat. Liam clenched his jaw.

"You sure you want to try that?" He looked down at the Shadow Elf's ash-colored arm, the white tattoos standing out against his skin.

"Shut up," the Shadow Elf spat. "You better end this now, or I will slit your throat. We'll see who wins this battle when your precious royal blood spills onto the ground."

Liam felt the blade dig into his flesh, and he elbowed the Shadow Elf in his stomach. There was a grunt of pain, but the blade barely moved. Liam clenched his fist around his sword's hilt, and the lightning radiated through his body and into the Shadow Elf.

The blade at Liam's throat dropped. The Shadow Elf convulsed with a cry as the lightning circulated throughout him. His organs burned and then his muscles, until the currents ate away at his bone and skin.

The remaining Shadow Elves saw this, and Liam could tell that their resolve wavered; they slowed to a stop and backed away. They raised their weapons above their heads in surrender. The Tryans watched Liam to see what he would do, if he would show mercy to the stragglers.

When the Shadow Elves saw that Liam merely glared at them, they lowered their hands, their shadowed faces draining of their will to fight. Only a couple dozen were left alive and they reluctantly backed away, making sure that Liam or the others weren't going to come after them.

When the elves saw that he stood his ground, they turned and joined the others in fleeing. They ran as fast as the wind, looking like nothing more than haunted shadows as they disappeared into the forest. The army camp was overthrown within minutes, and every Shadow Elf had either fled back toward Nostfar or lay dead on the grassy field.

"WE LOST THREE," Rowe reported to Liam. He stopped a few feet from Midnight and looked up at the prince. Liam kept his face absent of emotion. He was captain of the Order. The title had been passed to him, and, at merely thirty-two, he was the youngest to ever earn such a title.

Liam lowered his sword, his eyes returning to a most crystalline blue that mocked the purest sea. The clouds began to part, and the sun shone its light onto the carnage that tainted the valley. Liam hopped from Midnight's back and bent down to a corpse.

Three losses out of a hundred weren't bad, but Liam felt partly responsible for those deaths. He was supposed to protect them. He sighed and nodded. All of those men were like brothers to him. He hated to imagine which ones had died.

"Offer them to the Silver River. May they have better luck in the Underworld." The men would be laid upon rafts and set ablaze before being sent down the river. It was a proper soldier's funeral. "May Lord Elahe bless them."

Rowe nodded and gave orders to Tuvin to take care of the task. The soldier gave a quick nod and hurried off. Rowe watched Liam for a moment as he knelt over a dead Shadow Elf, staring at it.

Liam rubbed the blackish blood between his fingers. He was in deep thought. He remembered the first time he'd seen a horde of Shadow Elves. It had been his fifth year in the Order, and they were attacked in the early dawn.

The Elves were like demons that stalked the night at speeds that left Liam and the other men on edge. Liam had almost been slit by a glowing dagger before his eyes could even adjust to their speed. The elf's maniacal sharp-toothed grin still lingered in his mind. He was thankful that Rowe had been by his side. It wasn't the first time that Rowe had saved his life...

"Liam?"

Liam looked up at his best friend and raised an eyebrow. "What?"

"Are you all right?"

Liam nodded and came to his feet. "I'm fine. Tired is all. I may have overdone it on the lightning." The other ninety-seven soldiers were gathered around him.

Rowe reached into his side pocket and tossed him a vial. Liam thanked him and popped the cork. A cloud of fog escaped, and he drank the liquid gingerly. He savored its replenishing waters.

Rowe waited for him to return the vial. He handed it to a passing fairy to refill it. The waters of the Silver River ran through Kyril and Alfheim, but only a fairy could bless it and encourage its rejuvenating properties.

"They managed to get a lot closer this time."

"Yes. I know. I can't understand how, though." Liam hated lying to his friends. He knew why, and the explanation was an impossible one.

The Guardians were awakened. They were the only ones who could open the doors to The Barriers. They had guarded and protected the doors for centuries, keeping the races safe from each other, keeping dark things from polluting the realms.

He wiped his hands clean on his pants. Liam stood tall amongst his kinsmen and cracked his knuckles. He spoke to them in a solemn tone.

"Gather all of the enemy bodies and burn them." His jaw clenched. This wasn't what he'd expected to see so soon. There had to be a couple hundred in this small force, but it was more elves than they'd ever seen.

"I don't want their stinking blood tainting our soil." The soldiers voiced their agreement; some spat on the bodies and went to follow their orders.

Liam looked up at the mountain that they had jumped from; it was massive, reaching toward the clouds. Its rocky terrain led down the valley and through the rushing Silver River. He had dreamed of such mountains when he was a child.

There was a time when he had been confined to the palace, when his mother, Queen Aria, had been too overprotective to let him leave the courtyard. She had held his hand when they visited other kingdoms, and his eyes had widened with wonder at the different landscapes of Kyril. He was grateful for her love and protection, but the day he had first picked up a sword had changed his life.

Rowe's approach broke him from his thoughts. The tall, brawny man came closer and spoke quietly. "What do you think this all means?"

Liam glanced at him and up at the sky. All of the storm clouds had vanished. "It means the Realm Wars have begun."

Rowe shook his head. "This is getting out of control. I don't even know if we're really helping. The Shadow Elves outnumber us at least ten to one."

"No matter. Like today, we will cut their numbers the best we can."

"Someone's a bit ambitious today," Rowe grumbled. "How long do you think we'll be out here? You know Cammie is going to give birth in three months."

Liam met Rowe's blue eyes and forced a smile. "I'll try to get you home in time to meet your new son."

Rowe returned the grin. "We can only hope it's a boy, but I'll be okay with a girl just as well."

"Maybe you'll have twins," Liam suggested, and Rowe gave Liam's shoulder a shake as he chuckled.

It was odd, hearing laughter when they were surrounded by dead bodies. He almost felt guilty for thinking of joyful moments right after a bloody massacre; as if he hadn't just revealed that, soon, they'd be fighting in a war that could go on for centuries.

Rowe's laughter died down, and there was a tense silence. Liam knew that distant look in Rowe's eyes. Neither of them wanted to say the obvious: Rowe might never return home to see his wife or unborn child.

Liam watched the fairies congregate toward the trees. He could see that they were saddened.

They had let three men die. A healer's job was never easy. They had to be entirely focused and ready, watching every man to make sure he didn't suffer from a blow that could prove fatal. Liam knew what pressure was put upon them. He shared that burden with them. They would beat themselves up over it for days.

Liam looked down at the grass. The battlefield was no longer green. The grass was brown now. Its life and energy had been sucked up and used by the fairies to heal the wounded soldiers.

Liam clicked his tongue and Midnight trotted closer. He smoothed the horse's flanks and laid his face close to his. "Good riding today, boy."

Midnight neighed in reply, stomping his hind legs.

Midnight was a stallion, both quick and aggressive. In battle, Midnight was agile, aiding Liam in his quick attacks as they weaved in and out of the masses. He was the most loyal and intelligent horse Liam had ever encountered, and he had trained him from a foal. Their bond was strong and pure.

Liam pulled a flask of water from Midnight's saddlebag. He drank the warm water deeply and handed it to Rowe. Rowe took a swig and sealed the top.

"We stick to the plan. It's off to Raeden we go."

Rowe nodded. "I still can't believe the elves are actually here."

Liam shrugged. "You'll see much more than just that if you stick with me."

"That better be a promise." Rowe clamped a hand on Liam's shoulder. "I'll get the men to hurry with the funeral pyres and the burning of the elves."

Liam gave a nod of approval. He wanted to tell Rowe what he knew, but he was too afraid of his own knowledge to put that burden on his friend. The world was about to change, and he was partly responsible for making sure it didn't plunge into total darkness.

He had immense power, but he sometimes wondered if it was enough. Despite his doubts, Liam refused to let his people down. He was driven by duty. It was his destiny, and he was a slave to it.

"Why the long face, pretty boy?" Nani teased as she hovered before him. Her glittering fairy wings caught the sun's rays so that he had to shield his eyes as he looked directly at her.

She smiled and landed onto the soft ground. He knew she was faking the smile. She was as heartbroken by the loss of the three soldiers as her team of healers.

Nani was a prodigy. No fairy village had known a healer as powerful as she, and she chose to follow Liam. She believed in him even if none of the other kingdoms and villages did.

Nani batted her eyelashes at Liam, bright green eyes full of affection for him. "You did well today. You showed the enemy a taste of what they're up against. A little flashy, but you know how I like theatrics, my dear prince."

Barely taller than four feet, Nani walked over to him, her deep purple pigtails bouncing with each step she took in her supple thigh-high brown leather boots. Nani ignored the stares of some of the men as she walked by. Her eyes were set on Liam.

Liam chose not to mention the dead soldiers. "Are you sure you're up for staying with this army? Things are only going to get worse. We are heading deeper and deeper into the wild lands to eliminate these Shadow Elves. It's going to be dangerous for you girls."

Nani scoffed. "I have the most powerful man in the world on my side. I think we'll be all right." She winked at him.

Liam grinned. "Not the most powerful," he corrected. "There are the 'others.'"

Nani turned up her nose. "I won't believe it until I see it."

"Talking about the Chosen class again?" Rowe stood with his legs spread apart. He folded his arms across his large muscle-bound chest. "I don't know why the Ancients won't just come down here themselves and set things straight. Save us all a load of trouble."

"There's a lot that you don't know, Rowe." Nani smirked. "Why don't you stick to your brutish ways and let Prince Liam do all of the thinking."

Rowe shrugged. "Works for me."

Nani laughed. "That's why I like you, Rowe. I think the safest place to be right now is by your and Liam's side."

What were the other Chosen ones were up to? Together they were supposed to unite the entire world and end all evil.

Maybe they could unite the races, but there would always be a new evil to conquer.

Sona stepped through the crowd. "Heal me," she demanded.

Nani flew toward Sona with a grin. "Say please." She flew away before Sona could push her. Nani laughed softly, nearly a child by comparison to the Tryan woman before her.

Nani flew closer and brought her face close to Sona's. This time, she mocked a serious expression.

"Getting a little sloppy." A twinkle filled Nani's green eyes. "I am not impressed."

Here we go, Liam thought.

"Just fix it, you little twit!"

Nani raised an eyebrow and spoke to Liam. "Whoa, lady!" She mocked a gasp of shock. "The manners on this one! Where'd you find her, anyway? A slum?"

Sona ignored her. She looked over at Liam as Nani's healing hands mended her swollen jaw. A yellow glow covered Sona's face, sealing the wound and decreasing the swelling.

"Done." Nani stepped onto the ground and curtsied. "My lady."

"Thank you," Sona said, though she sneered and turned on her heels to walk away. She wrapped her arms around Liam's neck.

Liam tensed, seeing the others eying them. "Not now, Sona," he said quietly into her ear.

She kissed his cheek and nodded. "Of course, darling." She glanced back at Nani. "Wouldn't want the fairy to get jealous."

Nani tossed her head back and laughed. She looked back at Sona. "Jealous? Of what? You can't even fly!"

Sona gave Liam another kiss, on his lips. "Good job today. You handled the battle well."

Liam watched Sona as she headed toward the other soldiers. She only let her hardened persona relax around him.

Liam sauntered toward the Silver River. It was the only body of water that stretched from Kyril to Alfheim, where the Silver Elves lived.

He listened to The Winds. They were unusually quiet lately. He missed their voices.

It was nice to know when danger was around, before it reached him. There was rarely anything exciting in the palace; however, when he had finally been sent away for his soldier's training, The Winds had revealed themselves with vigor each time he was in a battle.

Liam ran a hand through his hair and knelt down to the riverbank. He absently picked up a few pebbles and tossed them into the water as he listened. It was as if the air grew dense, and every other noise was muted.

He looked back into the direction of the camp. He wondered how many more he would lose before he was able to return home. What his mother had led the people of Oren to believe was a simple mission to rid the lands of a few rogue elves was something much more serious.

Liam felt something dark and evil approaching. The Ancients are warring, what does that mean to their creations? He shuddered. What would they do if their creators abandoned them? What would be the point of fighting if that happened?

Stop it, Liam, he sighed. You really do worry too much.

He turned to head back toward Midnight when he heard yells from the forest.

"Wait! Prince Liam!" Jonev, one of the sentries, shouted.

Liam felt his skin crawl with dread when the ground began to shake as something ran toward them. Liam's jaw tensed. Something was approaching. Something... big.

Jonev ran behind Liam, his eyes wide as he pointed toward the forest. "The elves, they set them loose!"

Liam swallowed. He had already used too much energy with his lightning skills. He took a long deep breath and rested his hand on the hilt of his sword. They were all watching him. The Order depended on him to lead. Liam refused to let those men and women down. They were his only friends.

Liam glanced over at Nani, whose smile completely faded. Her olive skin paled as she stared past him with wide eyes.

"Nani," he called. He drew his sword. "Get ready to work."

ABOUT THE AUTHOR

K.N. Lee is a New York Times and USA Today bestselling author who resides in Charlotte, North Carolina. When she is not writing twisted tales, fantasy novels, and dark poetry, she does a great deal of traveling and promotes other authors. Wannabe rockstar, foreign language enthusiast, and anime geek, K.N. Lee also enjoys helping others reach their writing and publishing goals. She is a winner of the Elevate Lifestyle Top 30 Under 30 "Future Leaders of Charlotte" award for her success as a writer, business owner, and for community service.

She is signed with Captive Quill Press and Patchwork Press.

K.N. Lee loves hearing from fans and readers.
CONNECT WITH HER!
www.writelikeawizard.com
www.facebook.com/knycolelee
www.twitter.com/knycole_lee
facebook.com/groups/1439982526289524/

ALSO BY K.N. LEE

THE CHRONICLES OF KOA SERIES:
Netherworld
Dark Prophet
Lyrinian Blade

THE EURA CHRONICLES:
Rise of the Flame
Night of the Storm
Dawn of the Forgotten (Coming Soon)
The Darkest Day (Coming Soon)

THE GRAND ELITE CASTER TRILOGY:
Silenced
Summoned (Coming Soon)
Sacrificed (Coming Soon)
Awakened (Coming Soon)

THE FALLEN GODS TRILOGY:
Goddess of War

Goddess of Ruin (Coming Soon)

STANDALONE NOVELLAS:
The Scarlett Legacy
Liquid Lust
Spell Slinger

MORE GREAT READS BY K.N. LEE

RISE OF THE FLAME (Epic Fantasy)
Six races. Four realms. One devastating war.
The survival of the universe rests on the shoulders of one human girl, but can Lilae escape slavery in time to save humanity?

NETHERWORLD (Urban Paranormal Fantasy) Demons, ghouls, vampires, and Syths? The Netherworld Division are an organization of angels and humans who are there to keep the escaped creatures from The Netherworld in check in this action-packed paranormal thriller.

Introducing Koa Ryeo-won, a half-blood vampire with an enchanted sword, a membership to the most elite vampire castle in Europe, and the gift of flight. If only she could manage to reclaim the lost memories of her years in The Netherworld, she might finally be able to move forward.

THE SCARLETT LEGACY (Young Adult Fantasy) Wizards. Shifters. Sexy mobsters with magic.

Evie Scarlett is a young wizard who yearns for an escape from her family's bitter rivalry with another crime family. But this time, she may be the only one who can save them.

Goddess of War (Young Adult Fantasy) Unsuspecting humans. Fallen gods in disguise. A battle for the entire universe.

After escaping the Vault, a prison for gods, twin siblings Preeti and Vineet make a desperate journey to the human world where they must impersonate the race they are meant to rule and protect.

SILENCED (New Adult – Paranormal Romance) Silence kept her alive. Magic will set her free.

Willa Avery created the serum that changed the world as humans, witches, and vampires knew it.

Liquid Lust (New Adult Romance) Sohana needed a fresh start.

Arthur--a British billionaire has an enticing offer.

Neither expected their arrangement to spark something more.

Discover more books and learn more about K.N. Lee on knlee.com.

54353161R00135

Made in the USA
San Bernardino, CA
18 October 2017